Bolan holster[...]
and leapt onto [...]

He hunched his shoulder and rammed the door. It flew open and hung from one hinge as the Executioner hit the floor and rolled to one side, looking up to see a lab-converted kitchen—and a man with an Uzi.

The warrior squeezed off a three-round burst from his subgun that lifted the hardman off his feet and dumped him crashing onto a table covered with test tubes.

Bolan rose to one knee as a guy wielding a riot gun racked the slide and raced in from the hall. He tapped his subgun twice, and six rounds flew from the barrel, driving the shotgunner against the wall. His head cracked plaster, dust billowing into the dim light as he slithered to the floor.

Sprinting to the front of the house, Bolan halted in the living room.

A tall, heavy man stood with his back pressed against the front door. He had a choke hold on a figure in a white lab coat, and he held a Colt Government Model .45.

"I will kill him," Ortez screamed, jamming the muzzle of the weapon into his prisoner's temple. "If you move, I will kill him!"

MACK BOLAN®

The Executioner

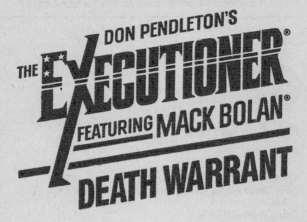

DON PENDLETON'S
THE EXECUTIONER®
FEATURING MACK BOLAN®

DEATH WARRANT

A GOLD EAGLE BOOK FROM
WORLDWIDE®

TORONTO • NEW YORK • LONDON
AMSTERDAM • PARIS • SYDNEY • HAMBURG
STOCKHOLM • ATHENS • TOKYO • MILAN
MADRID • WARSAW • BUDAPEST • AUCKLAND

First edition April 1994.

ISBN 0-373-61184-6

Special thanks and acknowledgment to
Jerry VanCook for his contribution to this work.

DEATH WARRANT

In doing what we ought, we deserve no praise, because it is our duty.

—St. Augustine
354–430

To some it seems an impossible task to stem the tide of illegal drugs flooding America's shores. But it's our duty to fight the battles, to do what it takes to keep the poison off the streets. There are major victories, minor setbacks. But the war on drugs rages on.

—Mack Bolan

To the courageous men and women
of the Drug Enforcement Administration

PROLOGUE

The sudden howl of the predator sent a cold chill streaking up Craig Waken's spine.

The DEA special agent watched the campfire. Flames danced from the low pile of brushwood, sending ghostly silhouettes onto the tall stalks of sotol and agave that encircled the camp. The howl turned to a succession of hoarse yelps.

Waken glanced at the other men seated around the fire. The U.S. Army special forces members of the DEA-led Recon and Arrest Team—RATs—all wore camouflage fatigues. Beretta 92-F automatic pistols were holstered on their hips. Each man's M-16 assault rifle lay within easy reach.

The RATs were ready.

Chanting human voices drifted faintly across the desert. Waken stared into the darkness to the east. The Papagos Indians were beginning their nightly sing, several miles away at the reservation. If they followed their pattern of the past three nights, the ritual would continue into the early-morning hours.

A voice across from Waken broke into his thoughts. "You in, G-man?"

The DEA agent turned toward Ron Bowers. A thin, regulation mustache ran along the burly sergeant's upper lip. Bowers held a deck of cards in his left hand. His right was poised on top, ready to deal.

Waken shook his head.

Static crackled from the field radio. "Control to A Team," a raspy voice whispered over the airwaves.

The rest of the RATs froze. Waken jerked the mike from the radio and raised it to his lips. "A Team— Control," he whispered. "Go."

"Target just dropped below radar. We've still got 'em on the homer, though, your vicinity."

"Roger." Waken thought briefly of Steve Kapka. The Paraguay-stationed DEA man had risked his life to clandestinely plant the homing device on the plane. Waken keyed the mike again. "B Team, you copy?"

"Affirmative."

Bowers had already risen and extinguished the fire. The rest of the men were sliding into the slings of their M-16s. Waken heard six rifle bolts slide home simultaneously.

The DEA agent rose and looped his own assault rifle around his neck. Habitually he pulled the 9 mm Glock 17 from the pancake holster on his hip and drew back the slide, making sure a round was chambered.

Silently he led the rest of the RATs through the heavy vegetation toward the landing strip. When they reached the edge of the cover, he halted them with an upraised hand. The men squatted in the stalks.

Behind him, on the winding wagon track that led from the highway, the RAT leader heard the sound of a truck engine nearing. He pressed the microphone to his lips. "A to B," he whispered. "Refueling vehicle on the way. Repeat—truck is here. We'll move in when they hook up. Cover us."

From somewhere on the other side of the landing strip, the voice came back. "Roger, A. *Be careful.*"

"No shit, Sherlock," J. B. Freeman whispered to Waken's side.

Waken didn't answer. In the distance overhead, he heard the faint hum of the twin-engine plane as it descended through the purple-black horizon. The DEA man turned to Bowers. "You double-check the floodlights?"

Bowers nodded.

The wheels of a twin-engine Cessna touched down at the far end of the landing strip. The plane slowed as it passed the hidden RATs, stopping at the end of the runway.

A two-ton truck nosed its way through the stalks and halted next to the aircraft. The shadowy outlines of fifty-five-gallon fuel drums appeared in the moonlight, tied to the truck's flatbed. A dark figure stepped out of the vehicle and walked toward the plane.

Waken reached in his pocket, producing the electronic transmitter. His fingers tapped nervously on the face next to the button as three men stepped down from the Cessna.

When the fuel hose from the first drum had been inserted into the Cessna's tank, Waken rose. He pressed the button on the transmitter, and suddenly the runway lit up. The men on the runway turned toward the light.

"DEA!" Waken yelled. "Freeze!" He stepped from the stalks onto the runway, followed closely by the RATs of A team.

Waken led his men quickly toward the Cessna. The four men on the runway continued to stare ahead, like deer frozen in a car's headlights. Two of the men had raised their hands over their heads. The other two used their cupped palms to shield their eyes from the glare. None of them appeared armed.

"Get your hands in the air—all of you!" Waken shouted, and this time the men turned toward the sound. "Don't move!" the DEA man repeated, and the men froze once more.

Waken moved closer. So far, so good. The drug smugglers were following orders. Everything was going well. Like clockwork.

The chill returned to the DEA agent's spine. Maybe too well. Something was wrong. He couldn't see it. He could feel it.

Craig Waken stepped into the light, his M-16 trained on the nearest man. It was then he realized what was wrong. The men were squinting against the lights, but all were smiling. The first shot caught Waken in the middle of the back. It felt as if he'd been rammed with a pile driver as the RAT leader's Second Chance ballistic nylon vest caught the slug. The M-16 dropped from his paralyzed fingers as he flew facedown on the runway. He tried desperately to roll to his side, but his arms and legs ignored the signals sent to them by his brain.

Waken twisted his neck and saw the muzzle-flashes of what seemed like hundreds of assault rifles. Four feet away, Ron Bowers went down, a round slicing through his throat, blood from the man's severed jugular jetting into the DEA man's face.

Concentrating hard, Waken inched his right hand up and wiped his eyes. As feeling began to return to his arms and legs, he reached for the walkie-talkie on his belt. "B Team!" he screamed into the mike. "B Team, don't—"

Another volley of rounds downed Freeman and MacDonald. Then Specklemeyer performed a dance of death as a steady stream of rounds entered his body. Waken dropped the radio as more automatic fire found its mark beneath the protective vest and speared through his legs, abdomen and groin. From deep within his throat, he heard a scream.

From across the runway came the chatter of M-16s. Waken opened his eyes to see Meyer, the DEA leader of B Team, and a half-dozen men in cammies sprint forward, firing. Meyer knelt next to him and grabbed him under the arms.

Waken was almost on his feet when several rounds burst through his savior's head.

The two men fell to the tarmac together.

Somewhere to the side, Waken heard Lee's voice. "Fall back!" Then another burst silenced the voice of the final man of A Team. The rest of B Team fled back to the cover of the stalks.

Sporadic fire soared over Waken from front and back as he lay helplessly on the runway. He closed his eyes against the red-and-yellow muzzle-flashes as the battle continued. Then, above the roar of the gunfire, came the whirl of helicopter blades.

Waken rolled to his back, looking overhead as the chopper descended. "Thank God," he murmured. "Thank God, thank God, thank..." Through the cobwebs in his brain, he wondered where the chopper had come from. *He* didn't remember requesting it. Had Meyer?

The helicopter dropped over the runway, its spotlight trained on the plane. Then suddenly the spot shifted, illuminating the remaining members of B Team as they crouched in the agave stalks.

Gunfire exploded from the helicopter as a dark shadow in the open door worked the mounted M-60 machine gun. More fire came from the hidden enemy across the runway.

A moment later six more bodies lay at the edge of the landing strip.

Waken waited, his breath coming hard as footsteps clattered toward him. The DEA agent's vision blurred as more of Bowers' blood dripped from his forehead into his eyes. A hazy form knelt over him. "The hombre still lives," the man called over his shoulder.

A dozen more obscure forms crowded around Waken as he wiped vainly at his eyes. Somewhere close by he heard the helicopter land.

A dark-skinned man in a khaki bush vest stepped forward. "So you are a RAT," he said. Leaning slightly, he prodded Waken with the barrel of the Uzi in his hands. "Do you know what we do to rats in my country? We shoot them."

Waken closed his eyes. Lightning-fast mind-movies of his mother, father, then his wife and twin daughters ran past his eyes as if a screen had been rolled down on the inside of his lids.

As if from somewhere in another world, he heard the voice again. "Should I shoot you, RAT?"

Waken felt his neck twist as he shook his head. "No," he rasped.

"No?" the voice repeated, chuckling. "Yes, that is what your former President had told you to say, eh? 'Just say no.'"

Waken heard the rest of the men laughing, then a cold, metallic thud as the bolt of the Uzi rammed home in the still desert night.

Behind his closed eyelids, Craig Waken saw a flash of red, yellow and gold.

But he heard nothing.

1

Lightning flashed. Thunder followed.

A dark figure stood in the entryway to an apartment building across the street from Miami's chic Le Monseigneur restaurant. The specterlike shape moved farther back as drizzle began to fall over the streets. Though he would have preferred to be dressed in one of his multipocketed, combat blacksuits, the man in the doorway knew the events of the night might take him out of the shadows, to where the sight of a warrior wearing combat gear would draw more than a second glance.

So he had modified his standard night stalker wardrobe. Hidden beneath a hip-length nylon windbreaker were a variety of weapons. Under his left arm, a suppressor-fitted Beretta 93-R rested in shoulder leather. A stainless-steel Desert Eagle .44 Magnum rode snugly in a holster on the man's belt. Opposite the Beretta, at the end of a sling, hung a Heckler & Koch MP-5 full-auto machine pistol. A half-dozen magazines had been stuffed into the pockets of the man's black jeans and shirt.

Through the drizzle, Mack Bolan, also known as the Executioner, studied the window of the restaurant. A short, swarthy man in a stylishly baggy, cream-colored suit sat facing the street. The top three buttons of his flaming red shirt were unbuttoned, and gold chains glimmered through the hair on his chest. He sat sipping champagne from a stemmed glass and looking intently into the eyes of the beautiful blond woman in the sequinned evening gown seated across from him.

The drizzle turned to a shower. Bolan watched through the fogging window as a waiter in white tie and tails set the check in front of Ricardo Marquez. The man in the red shirt glanced at it, then pulled a credit card from his wallet, and the waiter disappeared from view.

Bolan let his mind wander for a moment, drifting back over the whirlwind events that had led him to Miami. He had already embarked on a mission, and had put in a routine call to Hal Brognola, his contact at the Justice Department and Director of the Sensitive Operations Group, based at Stony Man Farm. The big Fed alerted him to the fact that two RAT teams had been ambushed in the Sonoran Desert near the Arizona-Mexico border. Brognola had been brief. The tip that a plane loaded with cocaine would arrive at the isolated runway had come from an informant in Paraguay. No, Brognola didn't know the informant's identity. The snitch had been developed by a Paraguay-stationed DEA agent named Steve Kapka. The man had kept his source confidential.

"It's obvious, Hal," Bolan had said. "You've got a double agent working here. Get me the name of the snitch, and I'll take care of it."

Brognola's voice had sounded weary when he'd answered. "Wish I could, Striker. Kapka caught a full magazine from a MAC-11 on the street in Asunción last night. Whoever his informant was, the name died with him."

Across the street Bolan saw Marquez and his date rise and start for the door. The Executioner stepped from the doorway and walked swiftly toward the Corvette parked at the curb.

The Executioner had finished his mission in a hurry, then hustled south to Miami, following the only lead Brognola had been able to provide: another DEA agent in Paraguay had found a notepad in Steve Kapka's desk. On the same sheet of paper where Kapka had noted the plane heading for Arizona, he'd written "Ricardo Marquez—Miami." Below that had been scribbled the words "cutting house."

Were the two notes connected, or just two isolated thoughts that had found their way onto the same sheet of paper? The Executioner didn't know.

But he intended to find out.

Bolan unlocked the Corvette and slid behind the wheel as Marquez and the blonde appeared at the door of the restaurant.

He waited while a valet drove up, exited a dark gray Mercedes and handed Marquez the keys.

The Executioner let them pass, seeing the blonde slide over next to Marquez behind the wheel. Giving them a block's head start, Bolan fell in behind. He cruised slowly through the light traffic, his eyes welded to the rear of the Mercedes. A faint glow stared back at him from the taillight on the right side of the car. Dull, shattered plastic gaped on the left.

The Executioner had "marked" the vehicle earlier, slipping into the parking lot to break out the taillight while Marquez and his date ate their salads.

Justice files, as well as Dade County Police records, had turned up an impressive rap sheet on Marquez. At forty-eight, the American-born Latino's pattern followed that of many successful criminals. Juvenile records being abolished when the offender turned eighteen, Marquez's first arrest on file had come a few days after his eighteenth birthday. Bolan knew this could only mean the man had begun his career in crime long before. Marquez's first adult arrest had led to an armed-robbery conviction, for which he'd served two years.

Released on parole, Marquez was back inside the walls on drug charges in less than a month. In the next ten years he had done time twice more, both times for the illegal distribution of controlled substances. And both times before he was thirty. After that the arrests continued, but convictions ceased. Several cases had been dismissed by the district attorney for lack of evidence.

That meant another thing to the Executioner. Marquez had found someone to pay off within the system.

After the age of thirty-five, even the arrests disappeared. Which meant yet another thing: Ricardo Marquez had gotten smarter as he climbed the ladder of organized crime.

Bolan followed the Mercedes through downtown Miami, up an access ramp to the highway. Marquez picked up speed as his tires hit the eight-lane highway, and the warrior settled back a quarter mile to his rear.

It wouldn't do to get spotted, Bolan reminded himself. He had no idea where they were headed, and if Marquez made the tail, he'd either lead the Executioner on a wild-goose chase through the city or try to ditch him. What he wouldn't do was lead him to the cutting house.

The rain retreated to a light mist as they drove on through the night. Finally the Mercedes's brake lights glowed red, and the vehicle pulled onto a ramp that led to a tract of condominiums. Marquez drove slowly past the first three buildings, then pulled to the curb in front of the fourth.

Bolan killed his lights, pulled into the parking lot and drove slowly around the corner of the building. Executing a quick U-turn as soon as he was out of sight, he nosed the front of his vehicle back around the apartment building.

From his vantage point, the Executioner saw the blonde's evening gown had been pulled down to her waist, and she stretched the tight garment back up to her shoulders, slapping playfully at Marquez's hands when he continued to fondle her breasts.

Soft, feminine giggles drifted from the Mercedes as the dealer and his companion entered into a final round of good-night gropes. Then the woman swung her trim legs out of the car and walked unescorted up the sidewalk and into the building.

Bolan followed the Mercedes back onto the highway. Fifteen minutes later Marquez pulled off again, into a middle-income neighborhood. The warrior cut his lights, creeping down the streets two blocks behind. The dealer turned into a housing development, passed a sign announcing Eastlake Patio Homes and followed a winding street past several rows of town houses.

The Executioner drew closer. Unless his hunch was wrong, the cocaine cutting house would be somewhere within this development. He'd have to make his move soon—locate Marquez's destination before the guy actually got there. If he allowed the man to pull into the driveway, any number of prying eyes might be watching from inside the house.

The Mercedes crossed a bridge over a man-made creek as Bolan continued to narrow the gap. Then suddenly Marquez turned right into a short cul-de-sac.

Bolan stepped on the accelerator, and the Corvette's powerful engine shot the car forward. Wherever Marquez was headed, it had to be one of the houses on this dead-end street.

The Executioner wouldn't get a better chance.

Marquez was halfway down the block when the warrior hit the brakes, sending the Vette into a slide of screaming rubber as it crashed into the rear of the Mercedes.

Marquez leaped from the car, his hand inside his jacket.

Bolan got out, weaving slightly. "Shorry about that," he slurred.

The dealer pulled his hand back out of his coat. "You drunk fuckin' idiot," he raged. He stomped menacingly toward Bolan, then his eyes flickered with indecision as he looked the Executioner up and down. He stopped a few feet away.

Bolan staggered forward. "Hey, lemme pay for the damage." He reached under the windbreaker. "I'll write you a check."

Marquez's eyes widened in horror as the Executioner's hand emerged gripping the Desert Eagle instead of a checkbook.

Bolan cracked the barrel across the drug dealer's temple. The guy's eyes rolled up under the lids as he slumped to the ground.

The drizzle continued as the Executioner glanced quickly to both sides of the cul-de-sac. Most of the houses were dark. If anyone had seen what had just happened, they weren't anxious to do anything about it.

Quickly Bolan parked both the Mercedes and the Corvette along the curb. Returning to the prostrate form on the pavement, he knelt, yanked an Auto-Ordnance Pit Bull .45 from Marquez's belt and stuffed it into his own waistband. Gripping the unconscious man under the arms, he dragged him to the Corvette.

Bolan slid a flexible "handcuff strip" from his pocket. Wrapping the plastic-coated wire around Marquez's wrists, he slid the notched end through the retainer and let it bite into the one-way teeth. The dealer's own belt bound his legs together. Ripping a strip down the front of the fiery red shirt, Bolan fashioned a gag, then laid Marquez facedown across the seats and closed the door.

Four town houses with common walls faced the Executioner from each side of the cul-de-sac. Two more sat at the end of the street. He could rule out the houses Marquez had already passed when the Vette struck the Mercedes. That left only the last two houses on both sides and the duplex.

Bolan reached under his windbreaker and swung the H&K MP-5 to the end of its sling. He walked quickly to the nearest house. Light shone behind the curtains in the front room. The Executioner knelt to peer through a crack between the drapes and window frame.

Facing the opposite wall, a chubby man wearing a bathrobe and argyle socks sat in a reclining chair in front of the television. Feet propped up, a bowl of popcorn in his lap, he munched excitedly as images raced across the television screen.

Bolan moved on to the adjoining town house. The blinds were drawn. No lights. Passing by, he crossed an open grass area that led to the next block. Making his way through a line of newly planted trees, he slid through the shadows to the duplex.

The residence to the right was dark. In the one to the left, lights glowed through closed blinds. The warrior moved quickly to the rear of the dark house, making his way past three bicycles chained to a firewood rack on the back porch. Creeping on toward the light of the adjacent porch, he squatted next to an air conditioner compressor by the sliding glass door.

The Executioner peered in to see a double bar-bolt in front of the curtains behind the glass. Indistinct silhouettes twitched through the rough cloth.

A small window was near the far corner of the house. Bolan moved swiftly below it, inching his head up and over the sill. More light radiated from behind the blind. The Executioner's gaze circled the window frame. The shades hadn't simply been pulled; they'd been secured. The dull gray sheen of duct tape showed faintly at the edges.

Whoever was inside didn't intend to be seen.

Bolan circled the house, finding the same gray tape on all the windows. He thought back to the sliding glass door. He hadn't brought a glass cutter, but even if he had, it would have been useless. The shadows moving about the room meant people, who would hear his scrapes long before he could cut through and unlock the bolt.

The windows were out for the same reason. For all he knew, armed men could be waiting in every room. He'd be dead before he was halfway inside.

The Executioner rounded the corner, returning to the front of the duplex.

There was only one way in.

The front door.

He gripped the machine pistol in his right hand as he walked quietly across the yard. An iron gate led to the front porch. It creaked eerily as he pushed through and crept silently to the door.

The Executioner's first kick rocked the door on its hinges, cracking the wood around the dead-bolt lock and sending dust and splinters cascading down to his feet. He kicked again, and the door flew from the frame into the living room.

Bolan followed it in.

A dark-skinned Hispanic sat on the couch next to the fireplace, a horse-racing form in his hands. Bright orange suspenders rode over his Mickey Mouse T-shirt. He looked up in shock as the door settled on the carpet, then lunged toward a revolver on the table next to him.

He never made it.

Bolan raised the H&K and tapped the trigger. A 3-round burst exploded from the weapon, splattering into the hardman's chest.

The warrior raced through the living room and down the hall. Behind the closed door to the bathroom he heard the shower quickly shut off. Stepping back, he had readied himself to kick when he spotted a portly form from the corner of his eye.

The Executioner hit the carpet as a blast of 12-gauge buckshot sailed over his head. Rolling to his side, he raised the H&K. Another burst of 9 mm parabellum rounds screamed from the muzzle, stitching into the face and neck of a fat man holding the stock of a sawed-off, double-barreled shotgun.

Bolan was on his feet again before the man hit the ground.

A Ping-Pong table in the center of the carpet served as the room's only furniture. Plastic freezer bags, gram scales, sacks of milk sugar and a huge pile of white powder sat on the dark green top. Three nude women stood around the table. They froze, staring in terror at the man in black with the machine pistol.

Bolan pivoted back toward the bathroom. His foot hit the door next to the knob, the hollow plywood splintering as it swung open.

A tall man dripping with water stood with one leg still in the combination shower-bath. He held a towel in front of him as he froze with one hand on the smoked-glass shower door.

Years of training in the jungles of Southeast Asia, as well as the more subtle jungles of organized crime and terrorism the world over, had sharpened the Executioner's eyes to the cutting edge. In a nanosecond he spotted the protrusion in the towel and fired.

Crimson spurted from the tall man's chest as a stream of 9 mms slapped wetly into his heart. He slammed back against the shower wall, the towel dropping to the tile.

A double-action Smith & Wesson 645 dropped from his hand, hit the inside edge of the tub, then slid around the rim like a basketball circling the hoop before finally coming to rest on the drain.

Bolan turned and headed back down the hall. Ducking, he burst into the smaller of the two bedrooms. Empty. Returning to the other room, he found the nude women still frozen in place.

He paused to catch his breath. Forcing the drug cutters, men and women alike, to work unclothed was routine. It cut down drastically on "shoplifting."

"Get dressed and stay put," Bolan ordered the women. He closed the bedroom door behind him.

Marquez was just coming around when the warrior reached the Corvette. Bolan yanked the belt from the man's legs, grabbed his bound arms and led him from the car to the house. "I've got something to show you," he said.

Marquez sputtered through the gag as he took in the carnage of the living room. His eyebrows rose high on his forehead in shock.

The man in the orange suspenders on the couch stared dully toward the door. His dead hand still reached for the revolver on the table. Marquez stared back, wild-eyed.

The Executioner dragged him down the hall, pausing briefly so Marquez could take in the fat man lying in the doorway to the bedroom. Then, pushing the dope dealer's head through the bathroom door, he pointed to the corpse sprawled on the floor.

"Take a good look, Marquez," Bolan said. "Then take your pick. You can die like whichever one you choose."

The dealer sputtered again, his face reddening as his eyes threatened to burst from the sockets. He fell to his knees in front of the toilet, his neck and head jerking spasmodically against the gag.

Bolan ripped the torn shirt from his mouth, and Marquez leaned forward, retching painfully into the toilet bowl.

The Executioner let him finish, then grabbed a handful of hair and jerked the man's head back. "Like I said, you can die however you want. Or you can talk to me. But talk quick. I'm not a patient man." He paused, letting it sink in. "I want your connection, Marquez, and I want it now."

The man's eyes flickered nervously toward the bathtub, then locked on Bolan's. He nodded. "The lab, it's in Paradise Key."

"Where in Paradise Key?" Bolan prodded.

"I'll... I'll have to draw you a map."

Bolan yanked him to his feet, then pushed him from the bathroom down the hall toward the kitchen. Pulling a Leatherman Pocket Multi-Tool from his windbreaker, he used the wire cutters in the pliers to snip the plastic cuffs.

Marquez rubbed his wrists, then opened the drawer below a coffee machine on the counter. Digging through a tangled mass of writing instruments, he came up with a pencil and a yellow legal pad. Quickly he sketched a route from Miami to the great "hammock" in south Florida.

"What are you going to do with me?" Marquez asked. "You said you wouldn't kill—"

"And I won't," Bolan interrupted. "I should, but a deal's a deal."

"Then what..." The drug pusher's words faded away.

Bolan spun the drug dealer around. He shoved him against the kitchen counter, slid another set of plastic cuffs around his wrists, then dragged him into the living room to the couch. Marquez's eyes widened again as he studied the dead man in the blood-soaked suspenders.

Tying the gag back around the dealer's face, Bolan knelt to replace the belt at his ankles. The neighbors had to have heard the shooting. Police would be on their way. He'd let them deal with his prisoner.

Marquez shifted on the couch as the Executioner looped the belt around his ankles. Bolan looked up to see the man's bound hands digging frantically into the back pocket of his slacks.

The dealer twisted suddenly and leaned forward, his wrists struggling around his back to his right side. Bolan saw a flicker of stainless steel in the man's hands.

The Desert Eagle leaped into the Executioner's hand, and a massive, semijacketed, hollowpoint .44 Magnum round drilled through the gag and out the back of Marquez's head in a flurry of blood, brain and bone. The cocaine dealer's eyes opened wide in disbelief, then closed as blood soaked the cloth in his mouth.

A North American Arms .22 Magnum "minirevolver" fell from Marquez's lifeless fingers to the floor.

2

Paradise Key lies a few miles southwest of the remnants of Homestead, near the southernmost tip of Florida. The hummock—or "hammock," in local parlance—rises like an island of tropical trees amid a sea of saw grass and buttonwoods. The trees—West Indian hardwoods—grow in a dense, mile-by-mile-and-half forest. Sections of the key are frequented by tourists, and within them can be found the park services building, several paved walkways, and thousands of forms of plant and animal life.

Few people venture into the other sections of Paradise Key.

Tropical birds sang through the darkness of early morning as Bolan left Highway 1 and turned onto Route 27. The deep, dank odor of the swamps rushed through the open windows of the Corvette to fill his nostrils. In the headlights he watched the green meadows at the sides of the road turn to the bristly teeth of saw grass. Here and there buttonwoods and red mangroves popped up within the scraggly confusion, and then the tall brown-and-green walls of the key appeared in the distance.

The Executioner cut to his parking lights and slowed as he neared the forest. According to the map, the cocaine lab lay several hundred yards through the dense vegetation to the east. Pulling to the side of the road, Bolan cut the engine and raised the hood. The lab wasn't far, and he shouldn't be long. Anyone passing on the dark highway would figure the Vette had broken down and the driver had gone for help.

Bolan walked to the trunk. Opening the lid, he dug through the mass of equipment until he found a wrinkled set of woodland camouflage fatigues and his web gear. From a small steel footlocker, he produced a pair of canvas jungle boots. Digging to the bottom of the locker, he found a Kem-lite and the ActionEar. The listening device and the thin plastic tube went into his fatigue pockets.

Bolan reflected on the stories he'd heard about Paradise Key as he trod through the thick vegetation surrounding it. It was regarded by Florida law enforcement as being second only to Key Largo Hammock in terms of danger. Within the dark, mysterious woods of both hammocks could be found modern-day pirates who ran drugs instead of gold, and occult practitioners who engaged in voodoo, *santeria* and any number of other ancient bizarre rites.

Often the bones of sacrificed animals were found in the woods.

Other times the bones proved to be human.

The Executioner stopped at the edge of the trees, peering through the night as he changed into the cammies. Death in the swamps could come in natural forms, as well, he reminded himself. Paradise Key was famous for its poisonous plants, and the most toxic of all was the manchineel. The sap of the "devil tree," as it was known, contained a poison so toxic that rainwater dripping from its leaves onto the skin could cause sores that refused to heal for months.

As Bolan slipped into his web gear and canvas jungle boots, he continued to stare through the darkness. A manchineel stared back.

Anchoring his jeans, shoes and windbreaker under a large rock, the warrior slung the H&K machine pistol over his shoulder. Twisting the Kem-lite, he heard a faint crackling sound as the glass broke within. Then a faint blue glow illuminated the immediate area as the chemicals within the tube mixed together.

Bolan threaded his way slowly through the dense trees, following the luminous needle of his wrist compass. Three hundred yards into the key, faint yellow rays of light shone through the dark leaves. Killing the Kem-lite, he moved on. The lights grew brighter. Sixty yards farther on, he came to a break in the vegetation and dropped to one knee.

In the middle of the clearing, on the other side of a stagnant sinkhole, stood a crumbling old house. A lone door, flanked by two windows, sat in the center of what appeared to be the rear of the building. Two men armed with MAC-11 machine pistols stood under the eaves lights, one at each corner.

Bolan pulled the ActionEar from his pocket and slipped into the headset. Training the microphone toward one of the windows, he adjusted the volume control, and a moment later an angry voice came from inside the house.

"Señor Reed," the voice said sarcastically, "it does not matter that you do not wish to cooperate with us. You have no choice."

"Let me go, Ortez," a second voice pleaded. "I'll keep all this quiet. You've got my word on it."

Raucous laughter echoed through the headset. Then a third voice said, "*Sí, hombre.* We have your word. But we feel much safer knowing that we have you, and your wife, as well."

More laughter came from inside the shack. Then the first voice spoke again. "I am sorry, amigo, but things are as things are." The Executioner heard the distinct sound of a cocking gun hammer. "Now," the voice went on, "get back to work or you will be killed. Then we will all have great fun with your wife. Before we kill *her.*"

The Executioner rose to his feet and shoved the ActionEar back into his fatigues. The man inside was being held hostage. His wife, as well. He'd have to keep that in mind as he planned his attack strategy.

Staying just inside the tree line, Bolan made his way swiftly around the pond toward the front of the house. Water ebbing from the sinkhole sloshed quietly beneath his boots. When he'd rounded the corner to the front he dropped to his belly. Standing by the rear door were two more men with machine pistols. One of the men wore a black sleeveless T-shirt. The other, in white, smoked a cigarette, the orange ember cutting a gleaming arch through the night as he raised it to his lips.

The Executioner released his grip on the H&K and slid the Beretta slowly from beneath his arm. Twisting the suppressor tight, he extended both arms before him and rested his elbows in the damp mud. The front sights of the 93-R fell on the man with the cigarette.

Bolan squeezed the trigger. The Beretta bucked softly against his hands, coughing out a single deadly round that entered the smoking man's temple and drove him back against the house.

A soft chuckle escaped the lips of his partner. "Pepe, what's wrong?" the man asked in Spanish. He reached forward, catching his falling comrade in his arms.

Bolan shifted the Beretta, centering the barrel on the man in the black T-shirt. The 93-R rasped twice more, both rounds drilling through the hardman's chest.

The warrior was on his feet and running before the two corpses had settled on the ground. Racing toward the front of the house, he transferred the Beretta to his left hand and lifted the H&K with his right.

One of the guards from the back rounded the corner. A 3-round burst sputtered from the 93-R, punching into the man's face.

Excited shouts flew from inside the house as Bolan raced past the falling body to the back. Drawing down on the second guard, he sent a steady stream of parabellum rounds rocketing from the man's waist to the top of his head. The guard's MAC-11 flew from his hands as he plummeted face forward into the sticky earth.

Bolan holstered the Beretta and leaped from the ground onto the back porch. Crossing to the door in two steps, he hunched his shoulder and hit the splintered wood. The door broke, flying open to hang from one hinge as the warrior hit the floor and rolled to his side, looking up to see the lab-converted kitchen.

And a man with an Uzi.

The H&K gripped in both hands, Bolan squeezed the trigger and pumped a 3-round burst into the hardman. Flesh and hair flew throughout the room, and glass crashed as the gunner fell over a table covered with test tubes.

From another room, a brief scream was suddenly muffled. Bolan rose to one knee as a short man wielding a riot gun racked the slide and burst in from the hall.

Three more rounds from the H&K sent him tumbling back in the direction he'd come.

The Executioner stood and sprinted down the hall. A man wearing an embroidered Mexican peasant shirt stepped out of an open door, a Weaver Arms Nighthawk carbine rising in his arms as he twisted toward the intruder.

Bolan tapped the H&K twice, and six rounds flew from the barrel, driving the man with the carbine back against the wall of the hall. His head cracked the rotting plaster and lath, sending dust floating through the dim light as he slithered to the floor.

Racing on to the front of the house, the Executioner ground to a halt in the living room.

A tall, heavy man with a drooping mustache stood with his back against the front door. Crouched behind a short thin man in a white lab coat, he had looped one arm around his hostage's neck. In his other hand he held a Government Model .45.

"I will kill him!" the mustachioed man screamed in heavily accented English. He jammed the barrel of the .45 into the temple of his prisoner. "If you move, I will kill him!"

"Ortez...please..." the man in the lab coat whispered.

"Shut up, Reed!" the man shrieked. He pushed the .45 harder against his prisoner's head.

Bolan let the H&K fall to the end of its sling. Slowly he crossed his arms, with his right hand inches from the holstered Beretta. "So what do you want *me* to do, Ortez?" he asked calmly.

The man's eyebrows rose in surprise. Like a dog who chased cars down the street, he'd never considered what he might do if he caught one. "Let me think!"

Bolan nodded. "Take your time." Hidden beneath his left arm, his right hand inched closer to the Beretta. "I've got nothing better to do."

"Shut up!" the man screamed.

Looking unconcerned, Bolan studied the situation. Ortez had been careless. As he spoke, he'd gradually straightened from his crouched position behind Reed. The man was a good six inches taller than his hostage, and Bolan now had a clear head shot at less than ten feet away.

If he could draw the Beretta before the man with the .45 pulled the trigger.

And if neither Ortez nor Reed moved at the last second.

Big ifs. Bolan felt the butt of the Beretta at his fingertips as his hand cased closer. All he needed now was a diversion.

He got it from the man in the lab coat.

Suddenly screaming in either bravado or terror, Reed leaned forward and clamped his teeth into the forearm around his throat. At the same time he reached up, brushing the gun down and away from his head.

The 230-grain .45 sounded like a cannon as it exploded. The shot angled down, slicing through the top of Reed's shoulder before lodging in the floor.

Ortez screamed as tiny beads of blood appeared on his forearm from Reed's teeth. He jerked his arm free, and Reed dived for the floor.

Bolan had the Beretta free of leather before Ortez could get off a follow-up shot. The 93-R coughed twice. The first round flew into the hardman's open, screaming mouth. The second shot hushed its way through the drooping mustache.

Ortez stared blankly at the Executioner, then collapsed to the floor in a heap.

3

His head propped against the headboard with two pillows, Coapac de la Rocha watched the sudden cloudburst beat against the bedroom window. The rain sent a warm, glowing sensation flowing through his chest. He had prayed to the sun earlier in the day, begging the god of the Incas to step aside for a moment and let the rain create the romantic atmosphere he would need that night.

And his god had listened.

Rocha took a sip from the champagne glass on the nightstand, then held a long, thick cigar to his lips. He drew in a mouthful of smoke, letting it roll over his tongue before releasing it. Without speaking, he turned to study the woman sleeping next to him beneath the sheet.

As always, their lovemaking had been magnificent. And as always, Josefa Pescadora had fallen into a contented sleep as she lay in his arms.

The serenity in Rocha's heart suddenly turned sour. He looked away, wondering briefly if Josefa fell asleep so easily with all of her customers. Forcing the painful image from his brain, he turned back to her. A long strand of inky black hair had fallen over her face. It rested on her closed eyelids, fluttering gently each time she exhaled.

Rocha continued to study the woman's face, trying to look past the wild strand of hair, through the closed lids to the pale blue eyes he knew they concealed. Josefa wasn't of pure Inca stock, as he was. At some point in her genealogy, one of her ancestors had mated with a European who had supplied the gene that had eventually culminated in her bewitching irises.

Josefa rolled onto her side, and the hair fell away from her face, the sheet from her throat. As Rocha stared into the cleavage formed by her breasts, his mind drifted back to their childhoods.

Coapac de la Rocha and Josefa Pescadora had known each other as children. They had both grown up near Cuzco, in the Urumbamba Valley of southern Peru, where the descendants of the Incas still lived. They had been friends, and during their teens, Rocha had fallen in love with the blue-eyed enchantress. But the future Josefa foresaw in the valley had seemed dismal. One morning when Rocha went to visit, the beauty's mother told him she had left during the night without explanation.

Heartbroken, Rocha left the valley a week later to seek his own fortune.

The young man's path had led him to the University of San Marcos. In his freshman year he had become involved with Sendero Luminoso—the Shining Path—a Peruvian Maoist group inspired by Inca mysticism. He had studied the writings of the great Inca historian Garcilaso de la Vega. And ironically it had been Vega who had opened Rocha's eyes to a simple fact, a truism that would shape the rest of his life.

Socialism didn't work.

Socialism killed initiative. The ancient Incas had lived under one of the first forms of socialism known to man. The kings had provided them with food, shelter and protection. But when the Inca leaders were killed by the Spanish, the people themselves became sheep without shepherds, quickly succumbing to their new masters.

No, Rocha had realized. In order to be brave, a man had to be free. In order to be rich, prosperous, happy, freedom was essential.

In order to take advantage of the system, stealing from the weak and manipulating the laws to one's own benefit, the laws had to allow such perversion.

From that time on, Rocha had continued to follow the ancient religion of his forefathers, praying daily to the sun and lesser gods. But he had dropped socialism like a hot coal in the hand.

Josefa's eyelids fluttered open, revealing the soft blue hue that sent the compassion flowing through him once more. The love in his heart threatened to burst open his chest. "You're awake?" he asked softly.

The woman closed her eyes once more. A moment later the steady breathing returned.

Rocha had left the university halfway through his second semester. Unable to find employment that would allow him to live in the new capitalist life-style he now preferred, he had drifted from city to city, country to country, taking to the streets to snatch purses, pull strong-armed robberies and sell *basuco,* the raw form of cocaine smoked by South American peasants. But still the young Inca had desired more, and his tall, six-foot frame and wiry muscles had finally landed him steady employment as a bouncer at Florentina's, the top brothel in Asunción, Paraguay.

In the brothel he had met two people who would change his life. The first had been Francisco Juarez, the head of the local crime syndicate. Impressed with Rocha's ambitious nature, Juarez had taken the young man under his wing, given him a job and allowed him to rise to the number-two spot in what was becoming a drug-smuggling operation that might some day threaten the Colombians for control of the cocaine trade. When Juarez had suffered a heart attack the year before, Rocha had stepped into his shoes.

The second person Rocha had met who would change his life was a beautiful young woman calling herself "Maria." But the Inca man had recognized her immediately.

Her real name was Josefa Pescadora. And to his horror, she had become one of the highest-paid prostitutes in Paraguay.

Josefa opened her eyes once more.

"I must talk to you," Rocha whispered. "You're awake?"

"Yes." Josefa smiled. Her eyelids fluttered seductively. "I rarely sleep with my eyes open, Coapac." She flicked the loose hair away from her face and rose to a sitting position. The sheet fell farther, to her waist, exposing high, firm breasts.

Rocha reached forward to fondle her. "Josefa, most of my life has been a struggle, but I've always gotten what I want. I've gotten it because I've taken it. Now I find something that I want. Your love, Josefa. Yet I can't force it from you as I have forced things from others."

Josefa's pale eyes flickered to him, then darted away. "You're always welcome here, Coapac. You may visit whenever you like. I will be here."

Rocha felt a snarl curl his lips. "Yes. Here." He waited for an answer. He reached for her breasts once more.

This time Josefa covered them with the sheet. "Coapac, we have had this conversation many times. I am what I am. Nothing will ever change that."

"I'll change it," Rocha promised. "You must come to live with me."

A hard smile thinned Josefa's sensuous lips. "Who are you to judge me, Coapac? Weren't you a thief before you came here?"

"I could find no other work."

"And *I* could?" Josefa asked, her eyes widening. "Yes, the wealthy businessmen of Paraguay are all dying to hire an Inca girl with no education."

"You aren't a whore at least, Josefa," Rocha said.

The woman's smile turned to a taunting grin. "No?" She held up her hand, flashing several diamond rings. "Look at my fingers, Coapac." She pointed to the open door of the closet where dozens of expensive dresses hung from the hangers. "Look at my clothes. I've done quite well for someone who didn't have her heart in her work, don't you think?"

Before he could stop himself, Rocha raised his open hand. The slap sounded hollow in the brothel bedroom.

Josefa stared at him without emotion. The rain drizzling down outside the window was the only sound. The woman's expression didn't change as her cheek began to redden. Slowly she rose from the bed and padded naked toward the bathroom.

Rocha called to her before she reached the door. "I will have you, Josefa. Someday I will have your love."

She turned gracefully, raising her hand to tap the red mark on her cheek. "Someday, perhaps."

"I *will* have you!" Rocha shouted. "It's my goal."

"Your goal is unrealistic. At least for now." Josefa disappeared into the bathroom and returned a moment later carrying her clothes. Turning her back to him, she took a seat on the bed and began to slowly roll a sheer beige stocking up her thigh.

"I have failed at nothing in my life. Do you know why?"

Josefa didn't answer. She slipped the other stocking up her leg and fastened it to the matching lace garter belt at her waist.

"Because my goals are always high," Rocha went on. "They always seem unrealistic to lesser men. You are my highest goal, but you aren't unrealistic. And I will reach you. Somehow I will reach you and prove my love."

Josefa snapped the other stocking to her garter belt and slid her feet into a pair of high-heeled pumps. "You have other goals, Coapac. You should concentrate on them." She stood and turned to face him. "Are you still flying to Tokyo tonight?"

"My meeting is in Taiwan."

She reached for her dress and pulled it over her head. "Yes, of course. I had forgotten."

Rocha smiled. "You could come with me. Then, when we return, I will have my men move you out of here and to the house in Green Hell."

Josefa's smoothed the wrinkles in her dress with the flat of her hands. "Coapac, your home in the wastelands would bore me to tears. Besides, if I hadn't been here, meeting men like Kapka, who would have warned you about the DEA trap in Arizona?"

Rocha bristled. "It's only a matter of time until I discover who the traitor is."

"But at least until then, my love, I should remain here where I can be of use to you. Besides, you want me only as a plaything. When you grow tired of me, I will be gone."

"No. Never."

"Then prove it to me, Coapac."

"How?"

"When your relationship with the Chinese is solidified, you will need someone you can trust. Someone who can establish the trade route to America and escort the first combined shipment. How much do you estimate the first shipment will be worth?"

Rocha eyed her warily. "Close to ten million U.S. dollars."

"Then put me in that position, Coapac. Let me escort the first shipment and give me the usual commission. I will put it away for a rainy day, in case you change your mind about your love for me. It will be a mere pittance to what you will make, and it will show me that you love and trust me. Then perhaps, I will leave this life and join you in yours."

Rocha felt the rush of adrenaline flow through his chest. Had he heard what he thought he had heard?

Yes. He was making headway. He had a chance.

"Button me up," Josefa demanded, circling the bed and backing toward him.

Rocha let his fingers trace the smooth brown skin of her back before he began fastening the snaps of her dress. "It's far too dangerous for you," he whispered. "I'll give you a million dollars when it's over."

"No. I'll work for it. If you give it to me, I'll still be a whore. Perhaps the highest-paid whore in the world, but still a whore."

Rocha reached the top button of her dress and felt the stirring in his groin start again. He reversed the procedure, opening the garment once more and pulling it to her waist. Turning her toward him, he cupped both breasts in his hands. "We are in no hurry, are we?" he asked.

Josefa smiled. "You're a good lover, Coapac. And, no, we are in no hurry."

Suddenly there was a loud rap from the hall.

Rocha looked up. Josefa turned toward the noise.

A second later the door swung open. Lopez plodded in, then the muscular bodyguard stopped in his tracks, his eyes glued to Josefa's naked breasts.

The women made no attempt to cover herself.

The man's lips fluttered in shock as he stared at the woman's nudity. His eyes filled with lust. Then those same eyes widened in fear as he realized the transgression he had committed.

Rocha grabbed Josefa's dress and yanked it to her chin. Blood pounded through his temples as he held the garment in place. "What is the meaning of this?" he screamed.

"I...am sorry, sir," Lopez stammered. "I didn't realize...and when I received the news, I felt that..."

Rocha's jaw barely moved as he said "Go on."

"Ricardo Marquez's cutting house in Miami has been attacked."

The blood in Rocha's head threatened to boil. He fought the desire to reach for the Detonics Scoremaster .45 on the nightstand and empty it into his bodyguard. "And for this, you break into my room and see the love of my life exposed?"

"But sir," Lopez said, "several of the men were killed, as was Ricardo."

"We have other men!" Rocha screamed. "And other cutting houses!"

Lopez turned his head to the side. "Sir," he pleaded, "I'm sorry. I saw nothing. I didn't see—"

"Silence!" Rocha roared. Then his voice lowered, becoming a soft, growling whisper. "I know your heart, Lopez. I know the real reason you chose to disturb us. It was to see my woman!''

Rocha grasped the Detonics in his right hand and leveled it at his bodyguard.

"Coapac! Stop this foolishness!" Josefa demanded. "I am a whore!"

Rocha looked at her, felt the rage in his heart intensify to the point where he feared it would crack. His ears rang as if a thousand bees and mosquitoes had invaded the canals. Turning back to Lopez, he pulled the trigger. The big .45 boomed against the walls of the small bedroom.

Lopez slumped to the floor, a gaping red hole in his forehead.

Rocha turned back to Joscfa and saw her staring at him in disgust. She shook her head wearily. "I am a whore, Coapac," she said. "For a hundred dollars, Lopez could have seen more than my breasts and done more than look."

THE MAN IN THE LAB COAT moaned as Bolan knelt and ripped his jacket and shirt away from the wound. The big .45 hardball round had entered through the back of Reed's trapezius muscle, exiting cleanly through the front. The hole was bloody, but the wound wasn't serious.

The Executioner studied the man for signs of shock. Sweat dripped from the bald top of Reed's head, matting the unruly brown-gray strands that grew long from the sides and back. The wild hair and the equally unmanageable mustache that hid both the man's up-

per and lower lips made Reed look like a bald carica-
ture of Albert Einstein. On the other side of Reed's
thick bifocals, Bolan could see his eyes.

Frightened. No, terrified.

But still coherent.

The Executioner pushed the torn shirt against the
bullet hole, applying direct pressure to stop the bleed-
ing. He placed Reed's hand over the makeshift ban-
dage. "Hold this tight," he ordered, "and lie still. I'll
find something to dress the wound." He rose and
started back toward the kitchen.

"Who are you?" Reed asked. "Are you the police?"

Bolan didn't answer. In the lab-converted kitchen,
he dug through a drawer by the sink, coming up with
a bottle of rubbing alcohol and several clean rags.
Resting on top of the refrigerator, he saw a large roll
of masking tape. Not as good as adhesive, but it would
work.

Some of the horror had left Reed's face when Bolan
returned to the front room. The Executioner dropped
once more to his knees and helped Reed out of the lab
coat and what remained of his shirt.

"Who are you?" Reed repeated.

"It doesn't matter. I'm going to get you out of
here." He soaked one of the rags in alcohol.

Reed suddenly directed his attention to the Desert
Eagle on Bolan's hip. "That's a big gun. I don't know
much about guns, but I find them mysterious. Quaint,
you might say. That's an automatic, isn't it?"

Bolan nodded and set the alcohol bottle on the floor.

"Can I see it?" Reed asked. "I'd like to see how it works."

Bolan didn't answer.

The man stared at the cloth in the Executioner's hand. "Will this hurt?" he asked.

"Probably."

Reed turned his head and began to softly hum "The Star Spangled Banner." The tune stopped suddenly as Bolan jammed the cloth against the wound. The man grimaced, tears forming in the corners of his eyes.

"How'd you get mixed up in this?" Bolan asked.

Reed winced again as the alcohol bit deeper into his open flesh. "I'm a chemist," he gritted through clenched teeth. "I teach at the University of Miami." He reached up, wiping sweat from the skin on top of his head. "My wife and I were—" He stopped abruptly, grasping Bolan by the arm. "Yes! My wife! In all the excitement, I'd forgotten all about her!"

"I know," Bolan said. "I overheard you talking to Ortez. They've got her, too, and we'll get back to that. Go on with the story."

Reed frowned. "How could you have heard us? We were talking before . . . before all this happened."

Bolan had no desire to explain. He already had a pretty good fix on the chemist's personality. Reed was scatterbrained, and his attention span was as short as an ant's leg. Some of that probably came from the shock he'd just experienced, but the Executioner would bet his last nickel that Reed had had a head start in the field of absentmindedness. The man in the lab-coat was no doubt intelligent. He could probably work wonders with test tubes, petri dishes and chemicals. But he'd have a hard time crossing the street by himself without getting run over.

No, if the Executioner told Reed about the ActionEar, the chemist would find it as mysterious and "quaint" as the Desert Eagle. He'd want to look at it, figure out how it worked.

And the Executioner had no time for such senseless pursuits.

"I listened through the window."

"Oh," Reed said. It didn't seem to dawn on him that the guards stationed outside might have had something to say about a stranger in full battle dress crouching beneath the windows.

Bolan dropped the bloody rag from the wound and soaked a clean cloth with alcohol. "Go on with your story," he directed.

"We were on our way through the parking lot after a night class," Reed continued. "At the university, I mean. I was walking Sylvia—that's my wife—through the parking lot when Ortez and two other men jumped us and forced us into their car at gunpoint. He had a gun—big, but not as big as yours. By the way, what caliber—"

Bolan pushed the clean rag against the bullet hole, and Reed stopped in mid-sentence. The Executioner began winding the masking tape over the man's shoulder and under his arm. "Got any idea why they picked you?"

Reed shrugged. "I was just in the wrong place at the wrong time. Ortez explained it on the way here. They needed someone to process a large load of coca paste they'd just gotten in. Their regular chemist had been killed by some Colombians, he said."

Bolan listened quietly as he finished taping the wound. It made sense. The Colombians had been the first to organize into cartels and take advantage of the millions of dollars to be made on Latin America's cocaine crops. But the savages of the neighboring countries hadn't been far behind. Now cartels in Chile, Bolivia and the rest of South America were springing up like weeds after a monsoon. The competition had bred violence, and gang-style slayings between competitors had become almost daily events. "So they wanted you to do the processing for them?"

"Yes," Reed said. "It's not difficult. Anybody with a rudimentary knowledge of chemistry could do it. But Ortez and his men weren't exactly Rhodes scholars. They weren't stupid, mind you, but they had no training in the subject. Their field of expertise appeared to be in dealing drugs, not refining them. That, and inventing new and unique methods of killing people." The chemist shuddered. "I've never met men like that before. So...barbarous." He stared up at the Executioner. "Have you?"

"Once or twice," he replied. "So you processed the paste into powder?"

Reed drew back defensively. "I didn't have a choice, did I? They had Sylvia and they'd threatened to kill her if I didn't cooperate. You must have heard that from outside the window.''

Bolan nodded. ''Relax. I'm not judging you. You did what you had to do. Any idea where they're keeping your wife?''

''Somewhere on Key Largo. That's all I overheard.''

The warrior rose, helping Reed to his feet. ''What can you tell me about their operation?''

The chemist shrugged. ''Not a lot. I've only been here two days. But I've overheard some things.'' He grinned mischievously, the wild hairs of his mustache falling raggedly over his teeth. ''They didn't know I speak Spanish.'' The grin suddenly faded, and he looked around the room nervously. ''There's...no one still here, is there?''

''No one who'll pay any attention.''

Reed nodded. ''I finished processing the other load of coca paste yesterday. It's already been shipped out. They were waiting for another.''

Bolan thought back to the cocaine he'd seen on the table at Marquez's cutting house. Twenty, maybe thirty kilos, tops. If it had been a typical shipment of paste, that would have accounted for only a fraction of the refined cocaine that Reed had processed.

The coke at Marquez's was now in the hands of the police. The rest would have been shipped to other cutting houses throughout the country. By now it might already be in the noses and veins of American junkies.

Reed bent to grab his shirt from the floor. Blood dripped from the soaked cloth, and he dropped it as if it might bite. His nose wrinkled. "I believe I'll see if I can't find something in the closet."

Bolan followed him down the hall. They came to the body still gripping the Nighthawk. Reed walked around the corpse as if he were a coiled rattlesnake. "I, uh, see what you mean about no one paying attention," he said.

In the bedroom Reed opened a closet door and began browsing through the hangers. "What they do, Mr.... What should I call you?"

"Belasko will do."

The chemist turned back to Bolan. "What they do, Mr. Belasko, is fly down using collapsible bladder fuel tanks. That way they don't have to refuel. Then they dump the bladders, fill the space with coca paste and fly back on the regular tanks."

Bolan continued to listen as Reed rambled on with mostly irrelevant information he'd picked up. The Executioner was already familiar with the collapsible fuel bladder procedure. It had become dangerous to refuel in South America. Besides increasing pressure by the various governments, impurities in the fuel meant a longer stay on the ground. The risk of discovery multiplied with each extra minute during the tedious process of filtering.

"When's this next shipment due?" Bolan asked.

Reed shrugged, his naked, skinny shoulders bobbing up and down. "Maybe today. Maybe tomorrow.

But soon." He turned back to the closet and pulled a large white dress shirt from a hanger.

"Let's get back to your wife."

Reed twirled back, his face flushing red. "Yes! Good Lord, in all this excitement, I'm afraid she slipped my mind again. And she's all I've thought about for the past two days, Mr. Belasko." The blush deepened. "I'm afraid in some ways I'm something of the stereotyped 'absentminded professor.'" His eyes fell to the floor as he slipped into the oversize shirt. "I'm rather ashamed."

Bolan grinned. Absentminded or not, he couldn't help liking Reed. "Don't be ashamed. Do something constructive to make up for it."

Reed looked up, his eyes widening in surprise. "Yes, certainly. But... what can I do?"

"Help me," the Executioner replied. "I intend to find your wife for you."

The chemist smiled.

4

"How do you know she's there?" Reed asked as the Corvette turned off Highway 1 onto Route 905A South.

"Trust me."

Bolan knew there was no point trying to explain anything as obscure as a warrior's "hunch" to a man like Fenton Reed. The chemist would never understand. Reed might be as scatterbrained as hell, but he was a scientist. Scientists lived by reason, logic. In their world of test tubes and formulas, two plus two always had to equal four.

Over the years the Executioner had found that the world he inhabited was never quite so black-and-white. And he had found that his hunches usually paid off.

There was nothing supernatural about them, Bolan believed. With experience came knowledge. The unconscious mind of a warrior with combat experience began to pick up clues, clues that didn't always surface to the conscious mind with complete clarity.

This time it was even more simple than that. There had been no landing strip in Paradise Key. That meant there had to be a point of entry into the U.S., one that was probably closer to the sea to avoid radar.

Add to that three facts: first Reed knew his wife was somewhere on Key Largo. Second the largest hammock in Florida was on the same island. And last the drug-smuggling operation had already taken advantage of the hammocks by hiding their lab in Paradise Key. Combine these things, and the "two plus two" added up to Key Largo Hammock.

Bolan kept the Corvette at the speed limit as he neared Card Sound Bridge, leading from the mainland to Key Largo. Traffic was almost nonexistent in the early-morning hours. The Vette crossed the bridge, then began wending its way around Barnes Sound. Dawn broke, and soon the high-rising West Indian hardwood trunks appeared on the horizon. Bolan pulled the car to a halt at the side of the road.

Turning to Reed, he said, "I'm going to leave you here. I don't know how long I'll be. Raise the hood like I did last night. If anyone stops, tell them help's already on the way." The Executioner glanced down at his watch. "If I'm not back here in four hours, drive into town and notify the police." He opened the door and swung his legs out.

"No."

Bolan turned back to him. "What?"

"I said no. She's *my* wife, Mr. Belasko. I'm going with you."

The warrior shook his head. "Reed, I don't want to insult you, but this isn't really your game. I think you know that. Do you love your wife?"

"Of course."

"Then stay here. You'll just be in the way. And you could get us all killed."

"But—"

"No buts, Reed. I'll make you a deal. You don't come along, and I won't help you teach your chemistry classes when we get you back to the university."

Reed bristled. His face turned red again. "I did all right last night, didn't I?" he said. "It was I who bit Ortez, wasn't it?"

"Yes, it was." He tapped the dressing on the chemist's shoulder lightly, and the man recoiled from the pain. "And it was you who got a bullet for your efforts. Now, stay here. I'll be back with your wife."

The Executioner closed the door behind him and walked to the trunk. Digging through the equipment, he lifted the Weatherby Mark V in its hard case, then hesitated. More than likely, this situation would be similar to the one he'd faced in Paradise Key. Stealth and silence would be the order of the day, and .460 Winchester Magnum rounds breaking the sound barrier didn't quite fit the bill.

Dropping the rifle back into the trunk, Bolan lifted a shorter, broader case. He flipped the hinges, and a Starfire II compound crossbow popped into view. Pulling the Simmons 4×32 scope from a side pocket within the case, he mounted it on top of the weapon.

Bolan heard an engine and he turned to see an aging brown Ford pickup truck coming up on them from the rear. Shielding the crossbow with his body, he busied himself in the trunk, keeping one eye on the road. He still wore the cammies, as well as the Beretta and Desert Eagle, but had covered both weapons with the black windbreaker. Bent over the trunk, he should look like nothing more threatening than an early-morning game poacher.

A young, Hispanic-looking man wearing a green, sweat-stained T-shirt waved as the truck passed.

Bolan waved back.

When the vehicle was out of sight, the Executioner slipped quickly out of the windbreaker. Yanking the H&K machine pistol from the trunk, he slid into the sling, then covered it with the jacket.

The warrior lifted the crossbow, closed the trunk and walked to the front of the vehicle. Reed had rolled down the passenger's window and sat with his arm resting out of the car.

"Anything else you can remember that might help?" Bolan asked.

Reed pressed a forefinger into his chin. The new sun on the horizon shown brightly on his bald scalp as his eyes stared at the roof. "There *was* something else I'd meant to tell you." His eyebrows lowered. "But for the life of me, I can't remember what it was. Must not have been too important."

Bolan nodded. "You can tell me when I get back." He took off toward the hammock.

Salt air from both the Straits of Florida on one side and Barnes Sound on the other blew lightly through the branches as Bolan entered the trees. The sun had risen higher now, and soft light filtered down through the thick branches.

He threaded his way through the trees. The foliage was even thicker than it had been in Paradise Key, and he silently cursed himself for not bringing a machete.

Sweat broke on Bolan's forehead before he'd traveled fifty yards. Once again the mosquitoes attacked in swarms. The Executioner's trained eyes darted back and forth, taking in every detail he saw. Somewhere within the ten-mile stretch of trees, bushes and shrubs, Sylvia Reed was being held hostage. But where?

The warrior continued to study the terrain, looking for broken branches, footprints, anything that might be a clue to her location. He didn't know exactly what he was looking for, but he knew he'd know it when he saw it.

An hour later a flash of metal caught Bolan's eye. Making his way through the branches, he stooped over and lifted a beer-bottle cap from the ground. Budweiser. Dropping the cap in his pocket, he began slowly searching the area in ever-widening circles.

Thirty yards to the east he saw the footprint. Barely visible in the thick grass around a gumbo-limbo tree, the toe pointed deeper into the hammock. Bolan followed the print. He passed a strangler-fig tree slowly choking the life from a thick oak, then more tracks appeared in the mushy earth.

Bolan squatted next to the footprints. The shoes had crepe soles. Stepping to the side, he compared the print to his own. Though the track resembled the Executioner's, it pressed a good half inch deeper into the mud.

The man it belonged to would be of heavy build and medium height.

The tracks led to a narrow road cut through the hammock. Grass covered most of the soft earth, but here and there tire tracks peeked out of the mud. Staying just off the path, the warrior followed it for a quarter of a mile before halting at a break in the trees.

Fifty yards away, in the center of the clearing, sat a rough-cedar, one-room cabin. Parked to the side was the pickup that had passed the Executioner on the road. On the other side of the shack, a short narrow landing strip had been chopped through the trees.

The Executioner dropped to one knee. The strip wasn't long, but it would be enough for a talented bush pilot. Pulling a set of pocket binoculars from the breast pocket of his fatigue blouse, Bolan held them to his eyes, focusing on the cabin. The structure had no back door, but two open windows stared back at him. Through one he saw a fat man with a double chin. The man sat at a table reading a newspaper. In front of him on the table were several empty Budweiser bottles.

The butt of a nickel-plated revolver extended from the shoulder holster on his left side.

Bolan trained the binoculars on the other opening. Next to the window, barely visible through the dirty glass above the sill, he saw the head of a woman. A ball gag had been shoved in her mouth and tied with a bandanna.

The Executioner shifted the binoculars to the side of the cabin. The thick forest grew nearer at the front.

Moving cautiously, he rose and made his way around the tree line to the side of the building, then dropped to his belly and crawled around the corner to the front.

A lone man stood at the front door. He wore a ragged red cutoff sweatshirt and cradled an Uzi in his arms.

Bolan considered his options. The light guard could mean only one thing. The shipment of cocaine hadn't yet arrived. As soon as it did, men would flood the area to protect it. And they might arrive any time.

For a brief moment the Executioner was tempted to wait for them. By moving through the trees, using first the crossbow and then his guns, he could rid the world of dozens of bloodsucking leeches, then retreat before they had a chance to pin him down.

But what about Sylvia Reed? Where would that leave her?

No, the woman's safety had to come first. He had to get her out before more gunmen arrived. Then, when there was time, he would come back.

Slowly the Executioner drew back the 150-pound bowstring, feeling the compound cables ease as he slipped it over the notch. Inserting a bolt, he rose to one knee and aimed through the limbs.

The man at the door stood less than twenty yards away. Bolan adjusted the scope's parallax objective accordingly. Squinting through the optical, he centered the cross hairs on the red sweatshirt and squeezed the trigger.

A soft whoosh sounded as the bolt flew through the air at two hundred fifty feet per second. The whoosh was replaced with a dull, wet thump as the steel shaft lodged squarely in the gunner's chest.

Bolan dropped the crossbow and leaped to his feet, sprinting from the trees toward the door as the man in red dropped the subgun. The gunner's mouth opened wide, forming a silent *O* as his bloody hands clawed frantically at the bolt impaled in his breastbone.

The Executioner heard the faint sound of a small plane descending overhead as he shoved past the dying man and shouldered through the door.

The man drinking beer at the table looked up from his newspaper in time to catch a 3-round burst of 9 mm rounds. The fast-moving parabellum slugs eliminated his saggy chins. His head shot back, then he fell forward over the table, sending the Budweiser bottles crashing to the floor in a flurry of foam and glass. Rolling off the table, the fat man's body fell into the mess, his crepe-soled shoes jerking spasmodically.

The driver of the pickup sat on a threadbare couch. Bolan twisted at the waist, stitching a quick stream of rounds into him as he lunged for an M-16 by his side.

A third gunman stood at the far side of the room next to a sink. He dropped the Budweiser can in his hand and scrambled for a stainless-steel Smith & Wesson 469 in his belt.

It wasn't even a contest.

Bolan's final burst started at the gunner's waist and moved up his chest. The man's lifeless fingers dropped the gun as he crashed to the floor.

Through the window, Bolan saw a Beechcraft Baron touch down on the landing strip and taxi to a halt.

Four men in white suits, all armed with Uzis, stepped out onto the runway.

Bolan turned to Sylvia Reed, getting his first good view of the woman since seeing her head through the window. A few streaks of gray coursed through her bobbed blond hair. She wore a knitted sweater around her shoulders. A wool blanket covered her legs.

The warrior's eyes narrowed as he suddenly realized what it had been that Fenton Reed couldn't remember to tell him. Just a small detail. Something of no importance that had slipped the chemist's mind— like so many other things did.

The Executioner glanced once more out the window as the four men started toward the cabin. He turned back to Sylvia Reed.

Her eyes wide in fear, the woman stared back.

From a wheelchair.

5

Bolan sprinted across the room to the woman. He kept one eye on the front window as he removed the gag from her mouth.

The four hardmen were halfway from the plane to the cabin.

"Who...who are you?" Sylvia Reed sputtered as the ball came out of her mouth. Her breath came in high, wheezing pants.

Bolan cut through the ropes at her wrists with the knife blade of the Leatherman. "We don't have time for introductions right now, Mrs. Reed." He ran back across the room, kneeling next to the man who'd driven the pickup. "If we don't get out of here quick, it won't matter who I am."

Fishing through the young man's pockets, Bolan came up with the key to the pickup. Rising, he hurried back to Sylvia's side and threw the window open behind her. Leaning down, he grasped the woman around the waist and lifted her into his arms. "I'm going to have to lower you through the window," he said. "Can you make it?"

Sylvia's terrified eyes shot to the front window. Bolan followed her gaze. The four men with the Uzis were now less than twenty yards from the front door.

Bolan shook her lightly. "Can you make it, Mrs. Reed?" he repeated.

The woman nodded slowly, and Bolan saw her shoulders stiffen with unshakable resolve. "We don't have much choice, do we?"

With the H&K dangling at the end of its sling, the Executioner lifted Sylvia to the window, maneuvering her limp legs through the opening. Then, grasping her tightly at the wrists, he lowered her to the ground outside.

To his rear, the Executioner heard heavy boots hit the front porch.

Holding the H&K tightly to his side, he dived through the window and over Sylvia as the door opened behind him.

There was a brief moment of silence inside the cabin. Then a voice said in Spanish, "Son of a bitch! No wonder they didn't come out to meet the plane!"

Bolan rolled to his feet. Staying out of sight beneath the windowsill, he lifted Sylvia again and hurried to the pickup. He deposited the woman on the passenger's seat and jumped behind the wheel. Inserting the key in the ignition, he twisted.

The ancient Ford engine whined, trying to turn over.

The warrior tried again, his ears pricked to the sounds of the starter, trying to gauge how much pressure to exert on the key. It had to start, and it had to start fast. The men inside the cabin would have heard the sound. In a split second they would recover from the shock of seeing their dead comrades and burst out of the cabin with Uzis blazing.

The Executioner twisted the key a final time, then kicked open the door. He was about to reach across the seat to grab Sylvia, when a flash of white cloth appeared at the back window.

An Uzi barrel extended through the opening.

Bolan caught the H&K's grip at the end of the sling and fired from the hip. A steady stream of parabellum rounds sailed through the window, and the shattered face slid beneath the frame.

"Hold on to my neck!" the warrior shouted as he positioned Sylvia on his back. Wrapping her useless legs around his waist, he clamped them close to his body with his left arm. Holding the machine pistol in his right hand, he began to back quickly toward the trees.

Sylvia continued to wheeze asthmatically, her breaths coming in short, tortured pants just behind his ear.

A second face appeared in the window, ducking just before the Executioner let loose a 3-round burst.

Bolan heard the front door slam as he reached the trees. Taking cover behind a thick oak, he watched as two gunners appeared at the side of the house.

The Executioner fired a burst in their direction, driving them around the corner to the front. The H&K ran dry, the bolt clicking open. For a moment there was dead silence.

Bolan slung the machine pistol and drew the Desert Eagle. He stared deeper into the trees. It had taken roughly an hour to find the cabin, but if he calculated correctly, he was less than half a mile as the crow flew from where he'd left Fenton Reed in the Corvette.

But that didn't mean he could outrun the remaining three cartel gunners. He had a woman on his back, and the men with the Uzis would know this hammock far better than he did. They might easily circle ahead and catch Sylvia Reed and the Executioner in a cross fire.

He could stay where he was and wait. But sooner or later the men would decide to split up. They'd come after Sylvia and him from different directions. If they had even a basic knowledge of jungle combat, they would approach quietly.

Bolan saw a quick flash of white at the side of the house and fired. The head ducked back as the Desert Eagle's mammoth .44 Magnum round sent chips of rough cedar flying.

No, there was no way he could win a waiting game with these men.

The warrior fired three more rounds from the big .44, making sure the men at the front of the house had pinpointed his position. Then, hurrying ten yards deeper into the trees, he fired again. Repeating the process a final time, the Executioner emptied the Eagle.

Bolan dropped the empty magazine, letting it fall to the grass, then shoved a fresh mag up the well. If any of the gunners had watched his progression, they should now have a fix on his direction of travel. The empty magazine at his feet would mark his path, as well.

Which meant it was time to change that path.

Staying twenty yards within the trees, the Executioner circled the clearing, moving to the opposite side of the house from the men. The warrior's trained ears strained for sounds of pursuit. If they came, they were drowned out by Sylvia's heavy gasps.

Reaching the other side of the house, the Executioner then followed the trees to the point closest to the landing strip. Lowering Sylvia to the ground, he reloaded the H&K before shoving the Desert Eagle back into his hip holster.

Bolan looked down at the woman. Her eyes were red and swollen. "Asthma?" he whispered.

Sylvia shook her head. "Just allergies," she gasped. "But they're bad." She hesitated, her bloodshot gaze falling to the ground. "I'm sorry. I know it's—"

Bolan pressed a finger against her lips. "Don't worry about it. Just keep as quiet as you can." He leaned closer, studying her. In spite of the physical disabilities the woman suffered, the Executioner saw a remarkable inner strength. "Try to hold your breath, Mrs. Reed," he whispered. "Just for a second, okay?"

Sylvia nodded. She took a deep, whining breath, then clamped her lips shut. The brave woman's eyes bulged slightly as her chest began to quiver in pain.

Bolan listened. From somewhere on the other side of the house, deeper within the hammock, he heard the crack of a dried twig.

Good. The gunman had followed the false path he'd laid out. They'd taken the bait.

Sylvia let out her breath, wheezing even louder after the strain.

The Executioner hauled her onto his back once more. Sprinting from cover, he crossed the runway and ripped open the door to the Beechcraft. He dropped Sylvia next to the controls and tightened the seat belt around her waist. As he slid behind the controls, he saw the large round metal drums stacked near the tail.

The Executioner saw no reason to waste time checking their contents. He knew what they contained. Coca paste. Hundreds of thousands, maybe millions of dollars' worth of death.

Piled next to the drums were four parachutes, a common practice these days. If American authorities tried to intercept smugglers in the air, the coke dealers simply put the plane on automatic pilot and jumped. While the air pursuit followed the plane, they made their getaway on the ground. The loss of large shipments was considered a hazard of the profession and could easily be recouped in the next few runs.

Unlike the pickup, the Baron started with the Executioner's first attempt. He stared through the side window, over Sylvia Reed's frail and shuddering shoulder, anxiously watching the trees as the engine warmed up. Depending on how deep into the hammock their pursuers had gone, they might still hear the Beechcraft and return, saturating the cockpit with gunfire before he could get the aircraft airborne.

As soon as he dared, the Executioner inched the control stick forward, turning the Beechcraft back toward the strip. Then, thrusting it full throttle, he raced the plane down the short runway toward the thick trees of the hammock. Waiting until the last second, he lifted the plane off the ground and high over the trees.

Bolan dipped the wing seaward, flying out over the water away from the hammock. Then, cutting back toward the trees below, he immediately began his descent.

Sylvia Reed was safe. But even now, the drug runners would be making their way through the woods, heading toward the road.

And Fenton Reed would be a sitting duck in the Corvette if they reached him before the Executioner did.

Bolan continued to descend over the thick foliage below. Seeing the road in the distance, his gaze fell on the tiny speck of black parked on the shoulder.

Fenton Reed sat on the Corvette's front bumper, staring into the hammock.

Bolan looked up and down the highway. Traffic had picked up considerably since early morning, and now vehicles of all sizes and shapes whizzed along its surface.

Maneuvering the controls, the warrior dropped the Beechcraft twenty feet off the ground and flew over the cars. Frightened faces looked up through the windows as he buzzed over their heads. Several of the drivers hit their brakes, pulling off the highway onto the shoulder.

The Executioner dipped the wing again, reversing directions. Repeating the process, he buzzed down over the traffic again. More cars took the hint, pulling to the side of the road as the drivers' frightened, angry faces stared up at the sky.

Circling over Card Sound Bridge, Bolan looped back and eyed the highway. The rest of the vehicles had gotten the idea. The pavement was clear.

The Beechcraft's wheels hit the highway between a Ford pickup on one side and a Datsun 300Z on the other. The plane bounced twice on the hard concrete, threatening to clip the Datsun with a wing before the wheels settled and Bolan got it back in control.

Sweat broke on the Executioner's forehead as he guided the wide wings of the Baron between the parked vehicles, scanning the road ahead until the Corvette appeared in the distance. Hitting the brakes, he passed the car and rolled another fifty feet before coming to a stop.

Fenton Reed still sat calmly on the front bumper.

Bolan idled the Beechcraft and leaped from the plane, pulling Sylvia after him.

The chemist looked up cordially and smiled, as if seeing an airplane land in the midst of southern Florida traffic was an everyday occurrence.

With Sylvia in his arms, Bolan hurried toward the Corvette amid a symphony of car horns and angry shouts. "Get behind the wheel!" he shouted to Reed.

The chemist jumped from the bumper and opened the driver's door.

Bolan placed Sylvia in the seat beside her husband. Looking up at Reed, he asked quickly, "You know the Crak'd Conch in Key Largo?"

Reed shook his head.

"Route 1," the Executioner said. "On the Overseas Highway."   Behind him, above the turmoil from the cars, he heard a rustling near the edge of the hammock. "Go straight there. Don't stop for anything. I'll meet you as quick as I can." He glanced at Sylvia. "Help him find it, Mrs. Reed."

Her chest heaving in spasmodic, rasping respirations, the woman smiled and nodded.

"Are we out of danger yet?" Reed asked.

From the hammock a long stream of automatic gunfire suddenly burst above the horns and angry voices.

"No," Bolan answered.

Whirling, he saw a white-suited gunner standing at the edge of the trees. Gripping the H&K in both hands, he peppered the hammock with 9 mm rounds. Red dots appeared on the subgunner's jacket, and the man slumped to the ground.

The warrior raced back to the Beechcraft and pulled himself into the cockpit. The other three men appeared at the tree line as he threw the stick forward. A moment later two rounds smashed through the aircraft's windshield.

Bolan increased speed, guiding the plane down the highway and into the air. In the side-view mirror, he saw the Vette pull onto the highway.

Good. The hardmen hadn't recognized the driver or his passenger in the confusion. And they'd had no reason to know the Corvette from any other car parked along the highway.

Air rushed through the shattered windshield as the Executioner headed higher, guiding the plane inland before banking back toward the sea. Continuing his climb, he dumped all but a few gallons of the fuel, then set the automatic pilot and walked to the rear of the plane.

He slipped the straps of a parachute over his shoulders, buckled the belt around his waist and stepped to the door. As soon as he saw the bright blue waters of the Straits of Florida in the distance, he opened the door and slid out.

The Executioner watched the plane head out over the sea as he fell through the bright Florida sunshine. It would continue on over the water, guided through the clouds automatically until the fuel was finally extinguished. Then, somewhere between Key Largo and Cuba, it would plummet into the sea.

Bolan pulled the rip cord. Air filled the chute, jerking him back up through the sky before he began to drift slowly back down.

The destruction of the Beechcraft would also mean the destruction of the coca paste it carried. The deadly chemicals the paste produced would never reach the brains and veins of the users in America. But the aircraft's cargo was just a drop in the bucket.

The Executioner's eyes drifted southward, toward Colombia, Peru and the other Latin American countries that grew the coca plant.

The fight had just begun.

BOLAN CROSSED the parking lot toward the screened outdoor porch of the Crak'd Conch. He had landed a half mile from Key Largo, hidden the H&K under a pile of rocks in a grove of palm trees, then made his way toward town, staying well off the highway. As he neared the city limits, the chances that a man wearing two guns and cammies might be seen and reported to local police had increased, and, as luck would have it, it was laundry day at the first house on the edge of town.

Slipping around the house to the clothesline, the Executioner had liberated a pair of olive green work pants and a matching shirt. The red-and-white patch on the right breast pocket read Texaco, and the name tag opposite it announced him as Ray. The pants fit fine in the waist and thighs, but they rode high on his calves as he mounted the steps to the restaurant. Buttoning the shirt had proved impossible, but that had worked out for the best, as well. By leaving it open over the T-shirt he'd worn under his fatigues, it provided cover for the Desert Eagle and Beretta. The green Texaco uniform might not get him onto the pages of *Gentlemen's Quarterly,* but it was functional.

Bolan crossed the porch, passing between the tables of late afternoon diners and drinkers who were taking advantage of the good weather to enjoy themselves outside. As on all of the southern Florida islands, dress on Key Largo was casual. Half of the Crak'd Conch's patrons wore shorts, the other half swimsuits, and Bolan's ill-fitting work clothes drew no second looks.

The walls of the main dining room had been papered with foreign currency and the business cards of customers. Bolan spotted Fenton and Sylvia Reed at a table next to a bar supported by vertical stalks of bamboo. They both sipped nervously on straws that extended from glasses filled with liquid, fruit and whipped cream.

Mrs. Reed sat in a wheelchair at the table. The Executioner frowned. That meant they'd ignored his orders to go directly to the restaurant, stopping somewhere along the way for the chair.

Sylvia dug through her purse as Bolan approached. She was breathing easier now, and Bolan saw her punch a tiny blue pill through its aluminum cover and pop it into her mouth. He crossed the room toward them, and the woman looked up, the strain on her face softening when she saw him.

The Executioner took a seat facing them. In the mirror mounted on the wall behind the table, he could still watch the door.

Fenton Reed wore the same smile he'd had on his face when Bolan had landed the Beechcraft. The warrior started to speak, but a waitress appeared. She set plates of cracked conch, chowder and fritters in front of the Reeds.

The waitress turned to Bolan. "What it will be?" she asked.

Bolan smiled. "Coffee and a big glass of water." When she'd left, he turned to the Reeds. "We've got to get you out of here. Someplace safe."

Reed looked up from his plate. "Can we finish eating first?" he asked around a mouthful of conch. "This is good." The chemist's face was a mask of innocence.

Sylvia hadn't touched her food. "Fenton," she said, "I think we should do what he says."

Reed shrugged. He took a bite of one of the fritters. "I don't see what the rush is. We drove into town all right. Even stopped at the orthopedic equipment store." He pointed to the wheelchair with his spoon. "Nobody's after us anymore."

Bolan shook his head. Reed was a likable sort, and he was too honestly naive to get angry with. But the chemist's innocence could easily get them all killed. "Just the same, Mr. and Mrs. Reed—"

"Please call us Fenton and Sylvia," the woman urged. "After all you've done, it's the least we can—"

"Okay. Fenton, I don't share your optimism at this point. These are bad men. Very bad men. I think you realize that from—"

Bolan saw the smile suddenly fade from the chemist's face, his spoon stopping halfway to his lips.

The Executioner's hand went automatically to the butt of the Beretta under his shirt. He glanced into the mirror to see a man wearing a wide panama hat enter the dining room from the street entrance. The man stopped in his tracks as he looked toward their table.

Reed whispered urgently, "I know him, Mr. Belasko! He's one of them!"

The man in the panama hat did an about-face and headed back through the door.

"Stay here," the warrior told them, rising. He gave the man a twenty-second head start, then hurried after him. He stopped on the sidewalk and saw the man in the hat a half block away, opening the door to a phone booth.

His hand still under his shirt, Bolan hurried to the booth. The man in the panama was dropping a quarter in the slot when the warrior jammed the Beretta through the door and into his ribs. "Don't move," he ordered. "Just come out quietly and walk ahead of me."

The man's hands rose automatically over his head.

"Get them down to your sides." The man dropped his hands and stepped out of the booth.

Holding the Beretta out of sight beneath his shirt-tail, Bolan ushered the man toward a nearby alley. If he could find an isolated spot, this new actor in the Reeds' continuing drama might be able to fill him in on more of the smuggling operation.

Shoving his prisoner into the alley, Bolan pushed him on toward a large white Dumpster.

Suddenly the man grabbed the brim of his hat and lifted it from his head. He turned toward Bolan, the hat held in front of him.

The warrior didn't need a blueprint to figure out what was happening. Things didn't always go as planned. He'd have to find out what he needed to know about the operation in Paraguay from someone else. He took a half step back and squeezed the trigger, the Beretta spitting two near-silent rounds of death through the hat and into the man's chest.

The guy's eyes opened wide as he fell to his face on the ground. As the panama hat rolled to the side, an American Derringer .357 Magnum slipped out of the crown.

The Executioner pocketed the gun and rolled the corpse onto its back. He quickly searched the pockets of the silk suit, finding several thousand dollars in a silver money clip, but no identification. The label of the suit read Antonio Cabras, Asunción.

Asunción. Everything kept leading back to Paraguay.

Bolan pocketed the money clip. He didn't know how well fixed the Reeds were, but there was a chance they'd need money while they waited for the protection he intended to get for them.

He lifted the body over his shoulder and dropped him into the Dumpster, tossing the panama hat in after him.

One more dealer of white death was now where he belonged.

6

The combination of modern streetlights and ancient Oriental lanterns hanging from the windows sent ghostly shadows dancing through the streets of Taipei, Taiwan. As the driver of the pedicab trotted along the narrow, winding route through the old section of the city, Coapac de la Rocha watched cyclists whiz past on paths flanking both sides of the street.

Rocha glanced at the man seated next to him. He had introduced himself as Mr. Hong upon meeting Rocha's flight. Short and thin, wearing a three-piece pin-striped suit and black horn-rim glasses, Hong was a stereotype of the Oriental businessman.

Bright neon flared from the cinema marquees, casting a spectrum of iridescent colors over the street. The signs promised both American and European films. Here and there between the cinemas were more subdued theaters, and drifting out of their open doorways came the piercing notes of Chinese opera.

Rocha watched the sights with a mixture of emotions. He couldn't deny the excitement he felt. Except for his early pilgrimages through South America as a pauper, he had traveled little. His wealth had come quickly, and in order to build his empire, it had been necessary that he remain on the scene to oversee its progress. Work had left him little time for pleasure, and now the sights and sounds of this strange, mysterious city filled his heart with an almost childish glee.

But mixed within the exhilaration, tainting it and preventing him from enjoying it to the fullest, was the anxiety that had settled in his chest after the last phone call to Cheung.

The man still seemed open to the plan Rocha had outlined, but he held reservations. He wondered if two "businessmen," as he called Rocha and himself, coming from such diverse cultures, could form a lasting bond of trust.

A light film of sweat formed on Rocha's forehead. He wiped it away with the back of his hand. He needed this arrangement. Compared to the large cartels in Colombia, Bolivia and Peru, his Asunción operation was nothing. Although he had recently begun smuggling cocaine directly to the U.S. on his own, it was still only a small part of his organization. The majority of his income continued to come from contracts to transport coca leaves for the cartels in Medellín and Lima. If he was ever to rise from mediocrity, to expand his enterprises to the next level, he would have to have the help of the Chinese.

Which meant he would have to convince them that he could fit into their way of thinking. And be trusted.

On the sidewalks sellers shouted the prices of embroidered tablecloths and towels, decorative bamboo screens and bird cages, baskets and ornately carved furniture. Above the chaos along the congested street, car horns honked, and stalled motorists raised their fists to one another in anger.

Rocha frowned, straining his memory, trying desperately to remember the section in his college world-history class that had dealt with the Taiwanese. Nothing came. Instead, his thoughts shifted to the few Orientals he had known at the university. Those in the Shining Path had been from the Communist mainland, and his principal recollection was that they had been naive, socialist idiots. He hadn't cared for their personalities or their looks.

He turned back to the busy activity in the streets as the driver raced on. He marveled at the sights and sounds. It was as if the Taiwanese had staged the whole show for his benefit. Half the people wore the traditional pajamalike clothing he associated with the Orient, drab, baggy suits of rough cotton or bright robes that bore the images of tigers, dragons and other beasts of Eastern mythology. But the rest were dressed much like Mr. Hong, or wore other fashions from the West. If he ignored their yellow skin and almond-shaped eyes, they looked as if they might have just stepped off the subway in New York or the underground in London. It was typical of the almost total fusion of East and West that Rocha had noticed since his plane touched down an hour before. Nationalist China had been as influenced by America and Europe as Japan.

Rocha took a deep breath, and his anxiety quieted. In light of all that, it seemed impossible that Cheung and his associates hadn't gotten used to foreigners who didn't fully understand their customs. Perhaps he would fit in after all. Perhaps he did have a chance.

For a moment Rocha breathed easier. He watched a pretty young woman hurry across the street, her head bowed in subservience. He thought of Josefa, so confident, so sure of herself. She was subservient to no one—not even to him.

A hot rush of heartache surged through Rocha's chest, mixing with the anxiety and all but killing the excitement. Josefa might be subservient to no one, but she *serviced* any and all who paid her price.

The pedicab slowed as a blue Toyota rounded the corner, skidding to a halt behind a stalled Honda. The driver of the Toyota leaned on the horn. His head shot out the window, and he let loose a long stream of what Rocha took to be Chinese profanity.

As the pedicab maneuvered around the confusion, the driver of the Honda replied. Extending his fist through the open window, he raised his middle finger, jerking his arm up and down in yet another concession to the West.

The pedicab finally stopped in front of a brightly lit nightclub. Two bulky Chinese men stood in front of the double doors leading into the building. Hong paid the driver, and both men stepped from the cab.

The two doormen bowed in unison as they stepped aside and opened the doors. Hong extended his hand, ushering Rocha inside.

The air of the crowded nightclub was thick with cigarette smoke. The dance floor in the center of the room was surrounded by tables occupied by men in tuxedos and women wearing evening gowns, diamonds and jade.

On the stage at the rear of the room, colorfully costumed dancers sang harshly in some primitive, aboriginal tongue. Their thick, flat swords flashed in mock battle, keeping time to the music of the archaic instruments in the orchestra pit.

Rocha followed Hong through the room, past the tables to a curtain. Hong drew it aside, and they passed into a dimly lit hallway. At the end of the hall another rugged, barrel-chested man stood guard in front of a door. A large, sharp-edged bulge marred the cut of his unbuttoned tux jacket. He looked up, saw Hong and turned to open the door. His coat fell to one side, and Rocha saw the glint of blue steel in a brown leather shoulder holster.

Hong led Rocha into a small, elaborately furnished dining room. Lanterns hanging in the center of the room cast a gentle light over the table. Red-and-gold mural wallpaper covered the walls, and in the dim illumination, dragons, lions and sea serpents seemed to jump from the paper into the room.

Several bottles of Tsing Tao beer littered the table, and the ashtray threatened to explode with cigarette butts. The two seated men rose as Rocha and his escort entered. Like Hong, both wore expensively tailored Western business suits. They bowed slightly, then extended their hands to Rocha.

"Mr. Rocha," the taller of the two men said as Rocha gripped his hand. "I am Mr. Cheung." Cheung was painfully lean, his skin stretching tautly across high cheekbones. His lips looked as if they'd been drawn on with a well-sharpened pencil. They stretched back in a smile, growing even thinner as they opened to reveal perfectly capped ivory teeth.

As the dealer shook his hand, Cheung went on. "Allow me to introduce my associate, Mr. Ling."

Rocha turned to the shorter man. Ling seemed the opposite of Cheung in every way. Short, corpulent and balding, he ran his tongue across fleshy lips, leaving them shining with spittle as he took Rocha's hand in his flabby paw.

"Shall we be seated?" Cheung said. He turned briefly to Hong, nodded, and the other man bowed and left.

A serving girl in a bright red kimono entered the room. Her hair had been tied on top of her head in a tight black bun. Her gaze remained on the floor as she stopped next to Cheung.

Cheung looked at his guest. "I have taken the liberty of ordering for you. You may have wine, or whatever you desire. Mr. Ling and I prefer beer."

"I prefer beer, as well."

The man's lips stretched back in a smile of approval. "I trust your trip from the airport was enjoyable?" he asked as the serving girl gathered the empty beer bottles and disappeared.

"Yes. Unique. I had never ridden in a pedicab before."

A low, raspy chuckle rose from Cheung's frail chest. "Yes," he said. "There are very few of them left. We arranged the transport in honor or your visit, Mr. Rocha.''

The girl in the red kimono returned, setting glasses and bottles of chilled beer in front of each man. Cheung waited until she'd left the room to speak again.

"Shall we drink to your visit, Señor Rocha, and the new venture we are considering?''

Rocha lifted his glass. "May it make us all rich," he said, and started to drink.

Ling interrupted. "We *are* rich. May it make us all richer.''

Rocha nodded and they drank.

The serving girl returned with steaming bowls of soup and intricately etched ladles. As soon as she left, Cheung said, "It is our custom never to discuss business while we eat. I understand that it is different in the West?''

"Yes," Rocha said. "But when in Rome..." He let his words trail off.

A quizzical look raised the eyebrows of both men seated across from him. "I don't understand," Ling said.

"It's an expression. 'When in Rome, do as the Romans do.' It means simply that we are in Taiwan. We will follow your customs, for which I have great regard.''

Both Orientals smiled. Rocha returned the smile, bowing his head slightly. Inwardly he chuckled. He had made points with these bastards, points he desperately needed. Rocha glanced down at his bowl.

Tiny fragments of what appeared to be grass floated on the surface of a broth. He was wondering what rare spice it must be when he heard a thunderous, sucking noise across the table.

Ling's ladle fell from his fat lips to his bowl, returning quickly upward. He slurped loudly, but stopped when he caught the disgusted glance thrown his way by Cheung.

Rocha took the cue and carefully raised his own ceramic spoon to his lips. It was already obvious that Cheung was in charge. It was the thin man's lead he would need to follow. Carefully wiping his mouth with the napkin, he smiled at Cheung. "Delicious," he said. "Please excuse my ignorance. May I ask what it is?"

"Swallow's-nest soup."

"Ah, yes. It's delightful." Rocha stuck his ladle into the liquid, trying to push the straw to one side. He wasn't successful, and several of the grainy reeds trickled back to the middle. Sighing quietly, he lifted a spoonful to his mouth and felt the coarse grass tickle his throat. Looking casually across the table, he saw thick strands of straw extending over the edges of Ling's ladle as the fat man gulped down another spoonful.

He needed to impress these men with his adaptability to their customs. With great effort, he downed the contents of his bowl, grass and all.

When the men had finished, the girl returned, setting a large plate of a scaly, fried substance in the center of the table. Rocha watched as Ling dug in, lustily ripping away strips of the food with the eyes of a man who hadn't eaten in days.

Cheung ignored him, eating slowly with precise movements and manners.

Rocha followed the thin man's lead, tearing off tiny pieces of the food and placing them between his lips, determined this time not to ask what the sickeningly sweet, fibrous substance might be.

When they had finished, Cheung looked up. "You didn't comment on this course. Was it not to your liking?"

Rocha forced a smile. "Please forgive my rudeness," he apologized. "It was perfect."

Cheung's showed his teeth again. "Wonderful! Westerners rarely like shark's fin."

Rocha fought the impulse to gag.

The serving girl returned and set plates of pork, beef, vegetables and fish in front of the men. Rocha recognized each dish and decided to comment appreciably on the taste without asking what ingredients they had been prepared in.

Ling ordered more beer, and they settled down to the main course.

When the meal was finished and the table cleared, Rocha waited silently, wondering if he should be the first to speak. As he waited, the door suddenly opened behind him, and a moment later a beautiful young Oriental woman in a sparkling blue robe slid onto his lap.

Two more young women, equally pretty, took seats in the laps of Cheung and Ling. Ling immediately pulled the robe off the shoulders of his "date" and began caressing her small, high breasts. He grinned across the table to Rocha as the woman in front of him stared indifferently into space.

Cheung slipped his hand inside the robe of the woman on his lap and looked up at Rocha. "Another of our customs," he said. "I hope it doesn't offend you?"

Rocha laughed. "Of course not. Again, it's a custom of which I wholeheartedly approve." He opened his woman's robe. He had heard of this custom from Japan. The Japanese influence, as well as that of Europe and America, seemed alive and well in Taiwan. While he would have preferred to have Josefa in his arms, the woman on his lap was beautiful.

"Let us get down to business, then," Cheung said. "You have proposed a joint venture in which we will exchange the smokable rocks of amphetamine we call 'ice' for your cocaine. Correct?"

Rocha squeezed the nipples of the girl on his lap. Though they were still hidden under her robe, he could tell her breasts were larger, more firm than those of Ling's woman across the table. "Yes, Mr. Cheung," he said. "But I propose more, as well. We will send combined shipments of ice and cocaine throughout the world, diminishing the risk factor for both of us by fifty percent." He paused, trying to read a reaction on Cheung's face. The man was noncommittal. Rocha continued. "Already ice is being shipped to the United States, and it has been readily accepted there. But it's being done by amateurs who haven't learned to take advantage of the tremendous market opportunities that men such as ourselves understand.''

Cheung nodded. His hand moved within the robe of the woman on his lap, causing the material to flap softly around her shoulders. "I understand. In China, as well as the other areas in the Far East under our control, we have a similar problem with cocaine. The drugs that we get, those that are of quality, are quickly consumed. The people are left hungry for more.''

"Exactly, Mr. Cheung. So more we shall give them.''

Ling bent forward, kissing the exposed breast of his woman. His lips opened, closing around her nipple, and a loud slurping noise, much like the one he'd made eating the soup, echoed throughout the room.

Cheung looked at him in disgust. "Mr. Ling..."

Ling straightened, sweat dripping from his flabby face.

"As I told you on the phone, Mr. Rocha," Cheung said, turning back to his guest, "my only concern was that our cultures—our ways of thinking, so to speak—were quite different. I have always had this picture in my mind of the South American gangster. He wears black leather clothing. He rides through the streets on a Japanese motorcycle, shooting people with a machine pistol. Then he returns to a filthy house to smoke crack and have sex with disease-infected whores.''

Rocha felt a blade slice through his heart at the word "whore." He forced himself to remain calm. Had Cheung done some checking up on him? Was he aware of Josefa? Had that last comment been meant to insult him, test him in some way? Or had it been nothing more than coincidence?

Cheung took a sip of beer and continued. "You are telling me that this is not the case?"

Rocha felt his shoulders relax. "I wouldn't mislead you. There are occasions when violence has been necessary."

"As it has with us at times."

"Yes," Rocha replied eagerly. "And we, too, have been guilty of stereotyping Orientals. We picture men dressed as Bruce Lee. They leap a dozen feet into the air, then kick each other. Or chop themselves to pieces with swords and hatchets."

All three men laughed.

"I assure you, Mr. Cheung," Rocha continued, "like your famed 'hatchet men,' the man you picture on the motorcycle is rare. He is used only when all else has failed, and he is far removed from the top levels of our business. We are organized well, Mr. Cheung, and the people at the top rungs of the organization are civilized men." He paused. "Like you and I." Rocha sat back and held his breath. He had played his trump card. Now the ball was in Cheung's court.

Cheung sat silently for what seemed like hours. Finally he said, "Mr. Rocha, you have convinced me. You are a man of great courtesy and respect." He turned in disgust toward Ling, who had bent forward once more to chew on the woman in his lap. "Some of our own people might take lessons from you."

This time Ling didn't notice the scowl.

Cheung turned back to Rocha. "We will do business, Mr. Rocha," he said. "We will flood Europe and the United States with both ice and cocaine, in quantities they have never before seen. And we will provide the people of China and the rest of the Orient with the same. Everyone, from Washington, D.C., to Beijing will have the drug of their choice. We will provide a service to the people, and all will be happy." He elbowed Ling in the ribs. Both men raised their beer glasses.

Rocha followed suit. "And as Mr. Ling so aptly put it," he said, "we rich men will become even richer. Let us drink to the new union."

When the toast was finished, the three women stood. "We have prepared a room for you upstairs," Cheung told Rocha. "Your hostess will accompany you if you like. If not, we can provide another woman...or a boy, if you prefer."

Rocha glanced at the woman who now stood at his side. Another sharp pain shot through his heart as he thought of Josefa, wishing it might be her who followed him up the stairs. Then the heartache turned to anger as he realized that even now she might be locked in the hot embrace of some sweating peasant who had saved enough money for one big night on the town.

Rocha turned back to Cheung. "Yes, thank you. But I like this woman." He slipped his hand up her robe and caressed her bare buttocks.

"Is there anything else you desire?" Cheung asked.

Rocha looked from Cheung to Ling, then stared Cheung in the eye. It had become increasingly evident that regardless of what place Ling might hold in the organization, Cheung was in charge. And he held the fat man in contempt.

Rocha knew he had already shown the Taiwanese his manners and respect. Perhaps this was the perfect time to show them his strength. "Yes, there is."

Cheung's eyebrows rose over the tight skin of his forehead. "Yes?"

"I would prefer two women tonight."

Cheung frowned, then glanced down at the woman at his side.

"No," Rocha said quickly, "she is yours, Mr. Cheung." He looked toward the woman next to Ling. "I will take her."

His host's skinny lips curled back in a smile. He grinned at Rocha, and in that moment a new understanding passed between the two men.

Coapac de la Rocha had made his place within the new organization. He was above Ling, equal to Cheung.

Rocha took the arm of the woman by his side and walked around the table to Ling's girl. Reluctantly the man dropped his hand from her breast.

"Have a good evening, Mr. Rocha," Cheung said. "We will discuss details for the first shipment in the morning before your return flight."

Rocha nodded. As the two women led him out of the room, he took a final glance at Ling.

The fat, former second-in-command looked like a baby who'd just lost his teething ring.

7

Bolan inserted the key into the lock of room 132, then reached in and flipped on the light. His warrior eyes scanned the room before stepping aside to let Fenton Reed wheel his wife through the door.

Reed took a seat on one of the beds while Bolan crossed the room to the desk. A beige push-button phone sat next to a prop-up cardboard advertisement proclaiming that the Green Turtle Seafood Market and Cannery canned five kinds of chowder, and proceeded to list them.

The Executioner punched the number that would get him an outside line, then the ones that would eventually link him with Aaron "the Bear" Kurtzman at Stony Man Farm. But first the call would be routed through several other numbers. To prevent tracing, the routing varied daily, and when a major op was under way, it sometimes changed hourly.

As the Executioner waited, Reed stood and walked across the room, drawing the curtain. Sunshine flooded the first-floor room. Directly outside, in front of the swimming pool, Bolan saw a shapely young woman in a black string bikini toss a beach ball to her toddler son. The boy missed the ball, his pudgy hands flailing wildly in the air, and it bounced over his head and struck the sliding glass door of the room.

The woman looked to be in her late twenties. Her honey blond hair had been permed into a mass of long curls, and it swayed in the breeze as she walked gracefully to the door and bent to pick up the ball. Full, sensual lips mouthed "Sorry" through the glass. Then she turned and jogged away.

Kurtzman's gruff voice brought Bolan back to reality. "Yeah, Striker. What can I do for you?"

"Several things. I'm holed up at the Holiday Inn Key Largo Resort. I'll be heading farther south. There's no point in running the whole thing down to you now, Bear—"

"Don't worry about it. Just tell me what you need."

"First I need everything you can round up for me on drug activity in Paraguay. We're talking coke, Bear, coming in from Asunción."

There was a short pause on the other end of the line. Then Kurtzman said, "Besides what Brognola's people came up with the other night, I don't recall much, Striker. Paraguay's always been a stopover for the coca leaves. The Colombians in particular route them through there from the fields in Bolivia and Peru. But they've processed it—at least as far as the paste stage—at home."

"I know that, Bear. I'm talking about direct smuggling from Asunción to the U.S. An organization that's grown big enough to pull off some fairly large shipments. You know what I'm talking about. Someone big enough to take out two RAT teams in Arizona.''

''Hang on.''

The Executioner waited quietly. On the other end he heard the click of keyboard keys as Stony Man's computer wizard searched his machine for leads. In his mind the Executioner could see Kurtzman surrounded by dozens of electronic devices.

Like Sylvia Reed, Kurtzman would be bound to a wheelchair for the rest of his life. The Bear had lost the use of his lower limbs when the Stony Man Farm had been attacked by renegade CIA agents several years before. But what Kurtzman had lost physically, he had gained mentally. Before the attack he was one of the best computer geniuses in the world.

After he could no longer walk, Kurtzman had seen to it that he became *the* best.

The computer wizard returned. ''There's not much here, Striker. I've got the usual number of small-time cocaine cowboys. Some ex-Nam vets turned bad. A few mercs moonlighting... but they're all once-in-a-whiles. Nobody flying out that could do it big-time.''

Bolan paused, thinking. Finally he said, ''Okay, Bear. Go back to what you said before, about using Paraguay as a routing diversion. Who runs that end of the business for the boys in Medellín?''

More keys tapped at the other end of the line, then Kurtzman said, ''Coapac de la Rocha. Ring a bell anywhere?''

''No, not offhand.''

"He took over the local crime syndicate in Asunción about a year ago when old man Juarez, that's Francisco Juarez, went out with a bad ticker. He's mostly a transporter for the cartels. Hey, wait a minute," the Bear said suddenly. "Let me try something else."

The computer keys tapped away again on the other end. "Well, not a lot here under unconfirmed Intel, either, Striker. But yeah, rumor has it he's trying to expand to direct shipment. He might already have."

"Thanks, Bear. I'll keep it in mind. Now, there's one other thing. I've got two witnesses here in the room with me. Fenton and Sylvia Reed. They're both potential corpses if they don't get some protection."

"Want me to get Brognola on the line?"

"Yeah. Set up a conference call. But before you do, is Grimaldi available?"

"He will be tomorrow morning. Right now he's got Phoenix Force on the way back from Puerto Rico. I can send another fly-boy if you need one right now."

The Executioner paused, considering the idea. Stony Man had other pilots at their disposal, and each was a crackerjack in the sky. But none of them was as good as Jack Grimaldi. The Executioner and the ex-Nam fighter pilot had done battle together more times than Bolan could count. They could read each other's thoughts almost as if they were both tapped into the same brain.

"No, tomorrow's good enough," Bolan finally said. "Whoever it is I'm looking for isn't going anywhere. Besides, someone needs to look after the Reeds until

Brognola can send protection. But tell Jack to gas up and meet me in the morning at Marathon Airport. I'll need some clothes, battle and civvy." The Executioner ran down a quick shopping list. "And tell Jack to bring me a chute. I'll be heading to Paraguay, and I don't care to explain to customs why I need all the equipment I plan to take in."

"Affirmative again, Striker. Let me put you on hold a minute, and I'll get Hal."

A moment later the big Fed came on the line.

"Brognola here, Striker."

"I'll let Bear fill you in on the details, Hal, but what I need right now is protection for two key witnesses who're in danger."

"You got it."

"Good. Send some men—make it three good ones. The Holiday Inn Resort, Key Largo. We've got adjoining rooms, 130 and 132. I'll be in 130."

"Good enough," Brognola said. "I can have them there in two hours from the Miami office. You'll stay with them until then?"

"That's affirmative. I'm grounded until Grimaldi gets back anyway." He paused. "Bear, I'll keep in touch. See if there's anything else you can scare up about the operation in Asunción."

"I will, Striker."

Bolan said his goodbyes and hung up.

IT WAS ALMOST six o'clock when the knock came at the door.

Bolan rose from the desk chair and drew the Desert Eagle from beneath his unbuttoned work shirt. He felt Fenton and Sylvia Reed's anxious eyes on his back as he crossed the room and pressed his eye against the peephole in the door.

Three men in dark business suits and carefully knotted ties stood outside.

The Executioner shoved the muzzle of the Desert Eagle against the door at chest level and reached for the knob. If the three men were who they were supposed to be, fine. He could have the big Magnum back in his waistband before they crossed the threshold.

Bolan cracked the door to the end of the chain. Without being asked, the nearest man raised a black credential case. He wore silver steel-rimmed glasses that matched his graying hair. His tanned face was all business as he said, "Special Agent Brett McFadden. These men are agents Chase and Bray." He hooked a thumb over his shoulder, indicating the men behind him.

Bolan glanced at the agents. Chase wore a thick brown beard, speckled with red and a few strands of gray. He looked like a heavyweight power lifter, with wide shoulders and hard muscles beneath a layer of fat. Bray was shorter, with long brown wavy hair and a mustache. A small gold stud gleamed from his left ear.

Reaching through the crack, the Executioner took the case. He glanced from the picture back to McFadden. The faces matched up. DEA IDs were almost as hard to forge as twenty-dollar bills.

But both could and had been counterfeited in the past.

"Who sent you?"

McFadden smiled. "Hal Brognola said you'd be careful. Our orders came all the way from the top, Mr. Belasko." He paused. "May we come in?"

The warrior closed the door, holstered the Desert Eagle and flipped the chain off the lock. Opening the door again, he stepped back and let the three men pass.

McFadden walked to the center of the room. "Fenton and Sylvia Reed?" he asked. Then, without waiting for a reply, he said, "I'm Agent McFadden. These guys are Chase and Bray. We're going to get you out of here to safety."

Sylvia Reed looked at Bolan, her face a mixture of anxiety and indecision.

The warrior smiled and nodded, and the woman in the wheelchair relaxed.

McFadden turned to Chase. "Bring the car around to the door at the end of the hall." The stocky man left the room.

Briefly the Executioner ran down the events at both hammocks. Then he, Bray and McFadden flanked the Reeds as Fenton pushed Sylvia out of the room, down the hall and through the glass door to the parking lot.

The dark blue sedan had so many antennae jutting from the hood and trunk that a six-year-old could have made it as "the Man." Chase took the wheelchair from Reed and pushed it to the rear door of the car. The bulky agent lifted Sylvia from her chair and placed her gently in the backseat. Bray folded the wheelchair and stashed it in the trunk.

Reed turned to Bolan and extended his hand. "I don't know how to thank you," the chemist said.

Bolan gripped the man's hand. "You're both alive. That's thanks enough." He couldn't suppress a smile and he couldn't help liking Reed. The chemist's haphazard approach to life had almost gotten the Executioner, Reed himself and his wheelchair-bound wife killed. But he couldn't really blame it on Reed. Different people had different strengths, different weaknesses. The brave ones did the best they could with what they had. And Fenton Reed had given it his all with what he had to work with.

"You told us your name," Reed said, "but you never really told us who you are."

McFadden, Chase and Bray looked curiously at the Executioner. Though they'd been given orders by Brognola to cooperate with the mysterious man known as "Belasko," Bolan could tell they were wondering, too.

"I did tell you who I am," the Executioner replied. "A friend."

Reed nodded, then shook his head. "Well, okay. But I'll always wonder. I mean, you've got the two guns. But it's like you should be wearing a black mask and riding a big white horse named Silver." He glanced at Bolan's open work shirt where the Executioner's guns were hidden. Reed's glasses slipped down the bridge of his nose, and he pushed them back.

"You don't happen to carry silver bullets in those things, do you?"

Bolan grinned. "Winchester Silver-Tips, sometimes." He opened the door. Reed slid in next to his wife.

Sylvia motioned to him through the window, and the warrior rounded the car to the rear door. The woman pressed the button, and the glass slid down. "Come here," she said, her tired eyes twinkling.

Bolan leaned down, and the woman kissed him on the cheek. "Thank you."

The Executioner watched them drive away, lifting a hand in a final goodbye.

JACK GRIMALDI LOOKED over his shoulder, his eyes hidden behind aviator lenses. "Five seconds, Striker."

Bolan slid open the Cessna's door and adjusted the piggyback chute, checking to make sure the backpack containing the clothing and other equipment Grimaldi had brought was secured. The Beretta and Desert Eagle hung in their usual places, and he'd slung a new H&K MP-5 over his shoulder. It could be partially broken down and stashed in the backpack when he hit the ground.

Grimaldi took a deep breath. "Go!"

The warrior leaped forward. The harsh wind carried him out and away from the aircraft as Grimaldi continued over the Chaco region of Paraguay. Silently the Executioner counted off the seconds before he'd jerk the rip cord, at the same time glancing down to see the city of Asunción to his left. The waters of the Paraguay River ran almost directly below. Though it was daylight, he knew there was little chance he'd be seen as he fell through the air. He'd be landing almost two miles from the city in the grassy plains along the river. And though it was hardly the HALO opening he planned, he'd be cheating considerably on the altitude at which he released his chute, giving curious eyes less time to spot him.

Coming to the end of his count, Bolan jerked the rip cord, simultaneously looking over his right shoulder to check canopy deployment. Without thinking, he began counting again. "One one-thousand, two one-thousand..."

The canopy shot out, started to flutter up, then drooped impotently behind him as he continued to plummet toward the earth.

The Executioner looked immediately to the release handle, arching his back to slow the drop. Grabbing the release handle, he looked back to the reserve rip cord, then jerked the release and sent the faulty chute fluttering away in the wind.

Below, the earth continued to fly upward toward him.

Bolan was less than three hundred feet from the ground when he grasped the reserve rip cord handle with both hands and jerked.

The emergency chute fluttered up over his head, spreading out like a giant wing to catch the wind and haul him back up into the air.

He breathed a sigh of relief as he began to descend again. Grabbing the steering toggles at the front of the rear risers, he pulled down and to the left, angling toward a grove of trees on the plain. As his feet hit the ground, he jerked the lines inward then quickly folded the chute into a tight square and headed for the trees.

Grimaldi had advised him that Stony Man still had no new Intel on Rocha, or anyone else who might be behind the RAT ambush and the new drug operation in Asunción. Which meant, as usual, the Executioner was on his own. He'd have to start from the ground level and work up, take each piece of information he came to as he climbed the rungs of the ladder toward the savages at the top, and try to make that piece fit into the puzzle.

The river dirt within the grove of trees was soft, and the entrenching tool cut through it quickly. When he'd dug three feet down, Bolan dropped the chute into the hole. Searching through the backpack, he found a ragged, faded pair of blue jeans, well-worn moccasins and a multicolored, Paraguayan sport shirt. Peeling off the blacksuit, he stuffed it into the pack and slipped into the wrinkled civilian clothes. Both the Beretta and Desert Eagle went into his jeans beneath the shirt.

Kneeling in the soft dirt, the warrior secured the Velcro closures of a Gerber leg sheath around his left calf. Made for a smaller knife, the rig had been modified at Stony Man to accept a Cold Steel Magnum Tanto with an 8 ¾ inch armor-piercing blade.

Partially disassembling the MP-5, Bolan stuffed the pieces into the backpack, zipped the watertight zipper and dropped it on top of the parachute.

The Executioner used the entrenching tool to fill the hole, then laid it on top and covered it with a thin layer of excess dirt. Rising to his feet, he wiped his muddy hands on the jeans.

A hard smile crossed Bolan's face as he turned toward the city in the distance and broke into a brisk dogtrot. Within seconds he'd worked up a sweat, making his shirt cling to his body.

He had neither showered nor shaved since the night before. Add these facts to his ragged, muddy clothes, and he should look like any of the dozens of other drug-using American ex-patriots by the time he reached the barrio section of Asunción.

8

The Executioner slowed his pace to a brisk walk as he reached the city. Taking Calle el Paraguay Independiente, he saw shawl-wrapped old women beating their wash on stones along the river. More women, these carrying black umbrellas clutched under their arms, rode sidesaddle down the street on donkeys, mixing in with the more modern traffic along the main thoroughfare.

Paraguay's government buildings lined the riverside. A handful of new structures sprang up amid the old French and Italian Colonial architecture. Bolan passed the marble walls of the Pantheon. Built by the impulsive and egotistical dictator Francisco Solano López during Paraguay's savage War of the Triple Alliance with Argentina, Brazil and Uruguay, the edifice still stood, reminding one and all of the man who had billed himself the "South American Napoleon."

Reaching the downtown area, Bolan spotted a bank. He hurried inside, exchanging several hundred dollars for Paraguayan *guaranis,* stuffed the bills in his pocket and moved on.

One of Asunción's ancient yet functioning trolley cars came to a rattling halt at the corner of the block.

The Executioner jogged over to it, paid the driver and took a seat on one of the aged wooden benches. He watched an old woman next to him roll a cigarette, then cut it in thirds with a rusty jackknife before jamming one of the stubs between her lips.

A group of teenage boys wearing the "colors" of the local gang got on at the next stop. They swaggered down the aisle in their matching jackets, doing their best to intimidate the other riders and prove their manhood. Cursing loudly in a mixture of Spanish and the native Guarani language, they took seats across-from Bolan and the old lady. The leader, a tall kid with a knife scar running from eyebrow to chin, initiated a staring contest with the warrior.

Bolan stared back, trying not to laugh. He watched the young man's expression go from tough, to uncertain, to afraid.

The kid's gaze fell to his feet.

Getting off at Padre Cordoza, Bolan cut down several side streets. Soon he had entered a section of Asunción visited by few tourists.

The barrio was a study in misery and hopelessness.

The mixed stench of stale urine, animal feces and unwashed bodies filled the Executioner's nostrils. Here, instead of colonial-era government buildings or modern skyscrapers, the dirt-packed streets were lined with wooden shacks repaired with jagged pieces of tin.

The blind, the lame and people with every other physical disability known to man moved listlessly about the squalid streets. Those who couldn't walk sat on corners, frayed hats in their outstretched hands on the off chance some passerby might drop in a few coins. An atmosphere of anguish floated through the air like a black storm cloud—a cloud that might only be misting for the time being, but threatened to explode in a thunderstorm of death and decay at any moment.

Several blocks farther along, the Executioner came to a stretch of fruit-and-vegetable stands, which eventually gave way to a series of cantinas. Here the poverty and corrosion remained, but it had been tempered with periodic rays of hope.

But that hope was cocaine.

Cleaner, better-dressed men circulated through the crowded streets. They stopped briefly at the sidewalk tables in front of the cafés, saying a few words to a patron here and there before leading that person into an alley or doorway.

Bolan watched the drug transactions as he moved along. You didn't have to be a DEA agent to figure out what was going on in Asunción's barrio.

Several Americans sat among the locals in front of a sign announcing La Cantina Viva. Bolan took the last empty table on the sidewalk, sitting where he could watch the street.

A dark-skinned waiter with a three-day stubble approached. He carried a sopping dishtowel over his arm and wore a soiled T-shirt bearing the picture of a boxing glove. Squinting an eye against the blazing noonday sun, he frowned down at Bolan. *"Cerveza"?* he asked.

"Sí, cerveza," Bolan answered.

The lukewarm beer came in a filmy glass. The waiter set it on the table in front of Bolan, took several of the stainless-steel coins the warrior dropped next to it and left.

Bolan took a sip of the beer and put it down. Looking across the street, he saw a man in clean gray slacks, *huarache* sandals and a shirt similar to his own. The man mingled through the crowd in front of another outdoor cantina. He was tall, healthy looking and had the handsome chiseled features of the local Maca Indians. He stood facing the Executioner behind a table, talking down to a young American woman with red hair. Each time he smiled, straight white teeth flashed in the sun against his dark skin.

The girl rose and accompanied him down a side street.

Bolan sat back, weighing the situation. It was the top of the cocaine organization in Asunción he wanted. But the bottom would lead to the top. And with no better leads than he had from Brognola or Stony Man, the bottom was where he would have to begin. Exactly *where* at the bottom to begin was the problem. Even the greenest rookie drug officer knew that the quickest way to blow their cover was to go in cold on sharp drug dealers. To the semitrained eye, the drug trade in Asunción appeared to be open. But that was a dangerous illusion to anyone who really knew the score. The redheaded girl and the other dopers making buys up and down the street had probably been regular customers for months, if not years. The street dealers trusted them.

And while the dealers always looked upon a new face in the crowd as a potential customer, they weren't stupid.

They also knew there was a good chance the new face was a cop.

Bolan took another sip of the tasteless beer. He continued to watch the streets as he planned his attack. He saw two more transactions go down at another sidewalk table a half block away. Then, as he was about to make his move, threading his way through the crowd in the hopes some hungry dealer would approach *him*, fate stepped in to lend him a hand.

The aging hippy who stepped off the sidewalk into the circle of tables in front of La Cantina Viva looked like a time traveler from the sixties. Long gray hair fell halfway down his back, and a matching silver beard hung lethargically from his chin. His blue jeans had been patched with everything imaginable—except denim—and the sleeves of his worn madras shirt were chopped off at the shoulders, exposing bony arms and nonexistent biceps. A bent and tape-repaired pair of granny sunglasses completed the outfit, which looked as if it belonged in the wardrobe department of the musical *Hair*.

The gray-haired man bounced slightly at the knees as his hollow, ratlike eyes scanned the tables, looking for a place to sit. When they fell on Bolan, the Executioner shrugged, then indicated the empty chair across from him with his hand.

"Thanks, man. I'm Eric." Eric hooked a ragged running shoe under the chair and pulled it back. Taking a seat, he extended his hand, grasping Bolan's in an ancient, upside-down "brother" handshake. His voice trembled slightly. "What's your name?"

"Mike," Bolan told him. He felt the man's sinewy fingers in his.

The waiter saw them and hurried up.

"Uh, nothing Carlos," Eric said. "I'm running a little short right now."

The waiter shook his head. "You no buy, you no stay." He indicated the street with a flick of his head.

Eric looked as though he might burst into tears. "Look, man," he pleaded. "I'll pay you later. First I got to meet this dude and—"

Bolan tapped the glass in front of him.

"Bring him a beer, Carlos. I'm buying."

Carlos shrugged and walked away.

Eric's wrinkled face twisted into a grin. "Thanks, man. I owe you one."

Bolan nodded.

Carlos returned with another grimy glass. Eric drained half the beer, then set the glass in front of him. "Better slow down," he said. "Soon as I'm finished, he'll be after my ass to move on again."

"Relax. Finish that one, and we'll have another."

Eric's eyes narrowed. "No shit? You got money, man?"

Bolan nodded. "Enough."

The hippy's head bobbed up and down. "Yeah, sure. I mean, I don't want to insult you or nothin'—"

his eyes ran up and down Bolan's tattered clothes "—but you don't look a hell of a lot better off than me."

Bolan chuckled. "Ran into a little luck yesterday. Scored pretty big."

Eric's head continued to bob. "Yeah, man. Way to go. Coke or weed?"

Bolan shook his head. If Eric thought his new friend "Mike" was already in the drug business, it wouldn't make sense when the Executioner wanted to be introduced to his connection. What's more, the way the skinny hippy couldn't sit still meant he was hurting right now and would probably want to buy from Bolan, which would get them nowhere. "No, not dope," the warrior replied. "I leave that to the big boys. I handle other things, if you know what I mean."

Eric nodded vigorously. "Yeah, man. I think I do. You look like you might of done some service time. Nam?"

"That's right."

"Yeah, me too," Eric said. "Then it's guns, right? You're runnin' guns."

Bolan said nothing. He let a big smile spread across his face and serve as his answer.

Eric downed the rest of his beer. "Figured as much. You're smart. Don't touch the dope, man. It'll fuck a man up good."

"Didn't say I never touched it," the Executioner answered. "Just said I don't sell it."

Eric's grin returned. His whole body bobbed up and down in agreement. "Right, man. I hear you. Little taste now and then never hurt nobody, right." Bolan saw a new hope in the junkie's eyes. "Listen, man," he said. "You holdin' right now?"

Bolan shook his head.

Eric looked nervously over both shoulders, then dropped his voice to a low, conspiratorial tone. "Listen, man, I know where we can score some *suco* if you're interested. But like I told Carlos, I'm a little short on bread."

Bolan nodded slowly. "Sounds good." *Suco* was the street name for *basuco,* a cheap, smokable form of cocaine that could cause total addiction after as little as one or two experimental uses. If Eric was smoking *suco,* it explained his near-frantic nervousness right now.

Combine that with the aging hippy's lack of funds, and it also explained why he was willing to take a risk with a stranger.

"So, what do you say, man? You furnish the bread, I furnish the connection." Eric's eyes looked fearful now, as if he was afraid Bolan might change his mind.

The warrior nodded again. "Fine. You know any women who might want to join us in a little toke?"

Eric was almost beside himself now. He thought he'd found the penniless cocaine addict's dream—a dope-smoking friend with money. "Man, I know where we can find the best pussy you ever had in your life." He paused. "Course, I gotta charge you just a little for that service, too. Not much. Just a little." He looked hesitantly at Bolan, and the Executioner could see he was wondering if he'd pushed too hard.

Bolan rose from his chair. "Let's go."

Eric led him away from the cantina, down a dirt side street to a row of dilapidated tenement houses. They crossed an alley, bent to crawl through a hole in a paint-chipped wooden fence, then mounted the steps to a garage apartment.

A fist-sized hole stared back at the Executioner from the glass in the top half of the door. The room behind the glass was hidden by a greasy, stained window shade.

Eric rapped loudly on the splintered wood, and a tiny shred of glass fell from the around the hole. The shade drew back, and a black face peeked through the hole.

The face wore a short goatee. The eyes above it were hard, dull, cruel. They gaped through the hole, first at Eric, then Bolan. A moment later the shade fell back in place.

"Go 'way, man," a deep voice said. "Nobody home."

"Come on, Alonzo," Eric pleaded. "It's me, man, Eric."

"What the fuck you think I am, Eric?" the voice said. "A motherfuckin' fool? Who the hell's this bastard?"

"He's a friend of mine, Alonzo. Man, what's the matter?"

"I tell you what's the matter. This friend of yours got 'policia' written all over his face. That's what the matter be. What happened, you get busted? Workin' off your debt to society by snitchin' to the Man?"

"That's bullshit, dude. I'm telling you, the guy's all right. I've known him for years. Come on man, let us in."

"Fuck you, man," Alonzo said. "And for *your* information, Señor Pig, I don't sell dope. Never have, never will, case closed. Now get the hell out of here. You can't do shit without a warrant, and if you had one, it'd already be in my hand and I'd be up against the wall."

Eric turned to Bolan. "Sorry, man. But I know Alonzo. He ain't gonna change his mind. But listen, there's this other dude I know, man. Let's go—"

Bolan shook his head. "No, Alonzo will do."

Eric's face looked puzzled.

The warrior wiped away the puzzlement by drawing the Beretta from under his shirt and bringing it down on the crown of Eric's head.

The Executioner caught the aging hippy as he slumped. Holding the frail form in one arm, he extended the Beretta in front of him and kicked the door. The glass remaining in the window shattered, and Bolan threw Eric through the door, then followed him inside.

"What the hell's goin' on?" Alonzo screamed. "Let me see your arrest warrant, you pigshit assho—"

The Executioner shoved the barrel of the 93-R into the screaming mouth. "Look down," he said. "Take a long, hard look."

Alonzo's eyes fell to the gun.

"This is my arrest warrant," the Executioner growled. "And unless you do exactly what I say, it'll be your death warrant."

9

The woman's breath came in fast, steady gasps. "Oh, God, oh ... yes ... yes ..."

She quieted suddenly, lying back against the sweat-soaked sheet.

The man on top of Josefa Pescadora lay forward, burying his face into the pillow next to her head. "I love you," he mumbled. "God help me, Maria, I *love* you."

"Yes," Josefa said, "and I love you, Alan."

The man called Alan rolled off her and onto his back. He slipped an arm under her neck and around her shoulders, staring wide-eyed at the ceiling, then crossed his other wrist over his eyes.

Josefa closed her own eyes as her head bounced lightly against Alan's arm. Oh, God, she thought. The tic. That abominable nervous tic. It might disappear when they were having sex, but it came right back like a faithful puppy dog as soon as they'd finished.

Alan breathed deeply, his air shooting down to make the hair on his chest flutter. "It's just... My God, Maria, I've never known anyone who could make me feel so..." He rolled to face her on his side, slipped his arm out from beneath her and propped his head up. "And it's good for you every time, isn't it? I mean, you're not just faking it?"

Josefa felt her lips fall into the well-practiced pout. She saw Alan tic twice and turned her face away. Reaching down between his legs, she pinched him. "Of course not," she purred. "You are a naughty boy to even suggest such a thing."

A broad grin covered Alan's face as he fell to his back. Then the grin faded and he closed his eyes. "We have to do something," he said. "I *want* you. All the time I want you. Will you marry me?" He opened his eyes and looked up pleadingly.

"I have promised you, haven't I? Is my word no good?"

"Of course it is. I'm sorry."

For several moments they lay there, lost in their thoughts. Then Josefa said, "What are you thinking?"

The man didn't answer at first. Finally he said, "Steve."

Josefa nodded, knowing he would feel the movement against his arm "Yes. I think of him frequently myself."

The man rose to his arm once more, staring at her. "I miss him. He was a good friend."

"Yes."

"And if it wasn't for him, I'd have never met you."

"That is true. He was a good friend to us both. Perhaps even more to me than to you. I'm sorry he's dead. But we must go on."

"I don't know how I'd have gotten through his death if it wasn't for you. My God, shot down in the street like a dog." He rose to a sitting position. Leaning over the side of the bed, he lifted his shirt from the floor, then dropped it again. "What we talked about," he said softly. "Your plan."

"Yes?"

"I don't know if I can go through with it."

Josefa leaned forward, hugging him around the waist and pressing her cheek into his chest. "Not even for me?"

Alan didn't answer.

"Think about it, my love," Josefa went on. "All I ask is that you think about it."

He stood up. "Do you want to take a shower?"

"Yes. You know I'll have to."

Alan's tic increased speed, and Josefa fought the urge to grab him by the hair and make it stop. The sorrow she saw on his face reminded her of Rocha. But Alan's pain was different, deeper. Perhaps it was because his love was true and unselfish. Perhaps it was because Alan was basically a good man, while Coapac was simply evil.

Josefa leaned forward, kissing him lightly on the shoulder. "Don't torture yourself, Alan," she whispered. "It's what I must do. For now. Soon it will all be over."

Slowly the man nodded. "It's just that it hurts so much, Maria. To think of you with someone else. Especially Rocha."

"I know. But it's the way things are. The way things must be." She paused. "Of course, if you decide you can go through with what we've discussed, it will no longer be necessary for me to remain here."

"I want to take you places," Alan said. "Nice places. Be seen with you. Watch other men's heads turn when we walk through a crowded restaurant. Watch them want you, and know they can't have you." He turned back to her, and this time his face looked like a little boy's. "Do you understand what I'm saying?"

"Of course," Josefa soothed. "It's what I want, too, Alan."

The man nodded again. The sad, lopsided grin she had come to expect from him at times like this appeared on his face. "I know you do." he said.

Josefa smiled back. "But there's only one way we can make it happen, Alan."

He looked toward the bathroom. "Shall we take a shower?"

"Yes. You go first."

The grin faded. "I thought we could—"

Josefa shook her head. "No. You go first. We must both return to work, and if we shower together—" she molded her lips and eyes into the calculated, mischievously sexy grin that always worked so well on him "—we might get distracted."

Alan laughed. "You're right." He rose and walked nude into the bathroom. A moment later Josefa heard the shower start.

The woman lay back, rubbing her face with her hands. She looked at the clock on the nightstand. Good. It was almost 12:35 p.m. He would have to hurry back to the office.

Alan came out a few minutes later, drying himself with a towel. He glanced at the clock. "We might have time for—"

Josefa's forced laugh cut him off. "Don't be silly. Do you want to risk ruining it all? You were late three times this week already. Your superiors will suspect something. It wouldn't do for them to find out you're sleeping with a snitch."

"Don't call yourself that."

"Isn't it what I am?"

He stared at her. "You're the woman I love."

"I'm both."

Alan dropped the towel and began to dress.

"I've hurt your feelings," Josefa said.

Alan's tic became more pronounced as he knotted his tie. "It'll all be over soon." Slipping into his sport coat, he reached into the pocket of his slacks and pulled out a wad of bills. Peeling two hundreds from the roll, he lay them reverently on the dresser, then moved back to the bed and bent to kiss her.

When he finally broke away, he stared into her eyes. "The money, it's for the information you give me, right?"

Josefa pouted again. "Would I charge the man I love to make love to me?" she asked. "You repay me for what I do with your heart, Alan, not your money."

He smiled, then he was gone.

Josefa rose and walked into the bathroom. Twisting the shower knob, she stepped under the hot, biting spray and scrubbed the man's odor from her body. God, how Alan disgusted her. But for the time being she would continue to open her legs for him. She would use him until she no longer needed him. She pictured him in her mind, his head bobbing away, and felt the nausca rise from her stomach to her throat. She concentrated on Alan's innocence, his good heart, and with the same detached, clinical state of mind as a scientist conducting an experiment, Josefa tried to force some small amount of remorse into her heart.

It simply wouldn't come.

She stepped out of the shower, wrapped a towel around her and walked to the dresser. Finding her brush, she stroked the black hair that fell almost to her waist. No, she thought, she'd known too many men, accepted too much money for her favors. Remorse and guilt were emotions that had disappeared forever many years ago. People, especially men, had used her far too many times for her to regret using them.

Josefa finished brushing her hair and went to the closet. She pulled a lightweight, conservative skirt and blouse from the hangers, then walked to the chest of drawers. Finding a black garter belt and stockings, she slipped them on.

She stood, slipped into the skirt and blouse and reached for the bottle of perfume on the dresser. She sprayed lightly behind each ear, then picked up the hundred-dollar bills.

Shopping. She would take the afternoon and go shopping with the money. She would buy some new clothes, respectable, conservative clothes like the ones she wore now. Dresses and skirts and slacks, the kind she would wear if Alan really did find the courage to carry out her plan.

The phone rang shrilly as she crossed the room. Stuffing the money quickly into her purse, Josefa picked up the receiver. "Yes?"

"Mr. Martinez is here."

Josefa sighed. She had forgotten. And regardless of how fat and repulsive Martinez might be, he was a regular customer.

"Did you hear me?"

"Yes, Anita." Josefa sighed. "Stall him a few moments. I had forgotten." She paused, glancing over her shoulder at the rumpled bedclothes. "Send Juana up immediately. I'll need fresh linen and towels."

Setting the receiver back in the cradle, Josefa walked to the chest of drawers against the wall. She removed her blouse and skirt. The bra and garter belt came next. Naked, she browsed through the top drawer until she found the slick, rubber panties and bra.

Leon Martinez was strange, but he paid well for his perversions.

Taking a seat on the bed, she sighed and began working the tight rubber panties up her thighs.

THE EXECUTIONER WHIRLED Alonzo around and shoved him against the living room wall. He jammed the Beretta into the base of the man's skull and ran his free hand around Alonzo's waistline, then up and down his legs. A long, thin bump hit Bolan's hand at the ankle.

The Executioner yanked a straight razor from the man's sock. "Planning to shave off your chin fuzz, friend?" he asked.

"You the only fuzz here, motherfucker."

Bolan grabbed Alonzo by the hair and threw him through the door to the bedroom. The man spun twice before coming to rest in a sitting position on top of a heap of dirty clothes. His eyelids rose in sudden realization. "Wait a minute, man," Alonzo cried. "You ain't no cop."

"You're the observant type, aren't you?"

"You here to rip me off?"

The Executioner didn't answer. Keeping the Beretta at the ready, he opened the door to the small closet, then dropped below the bare mattress to look under the bed. Besides Eric, unconscious in the next room, they were alone.

On the bed stand, Bolan saw a small quantity of *basuco* in a tin coffee can. Scooping it up, he held it under his gun arm and grabbed Alonzo by the scruff of the neck, dragging him into the bathroom. The Executioner handed his prisoner the coffee can. "Flush it," he ordered.

"Man, there's two thousand bucks' worth in there," Alonzo pleaded. "We can split it, man. We can—"

"I don't like to repeat myself," Bolan said in a graveyard voice.

With the look of a boy whose dog's just been run over by a car, Alonzo began to scoop the drug into the toilet bowl.

Reaching up, the Executioner pulled the rusty chain. The ancient, filthy mechanism coughed and sputtered as it flushed. Half the smokable cocaine disappeared. The rest floated on the water as the bowl began to fill once more.

"Try again," Bolan suggested.

It took three flushes before Alonzo's stash was no more than memories. Bolan dragged the man back to the living room and dropped him next to Eric. "You're going to take me to your connection, Alonzo."

Fear shot through the drug dealer's eyes. "Oh no! If I do that, the dude'll kill my ass sure, man."

Bolan squatted next to him and rested the Beretta on the bridge of Alonzo's nose. "*This* dude'll kill you sure if you don't, *man.*"

Alonzo tried to focus on the gun barrel on his nose, his bloodshot eyes crossing comically in the process.

Eric stirred next to them, then opened his eyes. His hands rose to the blood streaking down his face. "Wow," he muttered. "What a rush."

Bolan reached over with his free hand and grabbed the gray-haired hippy's collar, jerking the man's face up to meet his own. "This is your free one, Eric. Your *one* free one."

Before Eric could figure out what he meant, Bolan's left fist jabbed out, rocking him back to sleep.

The Executioner turned back to Alonzo. "Make up your mind. You want to die later, or now?" He tapped the Beretta on the end of Alonzo's nose.

The man didn't hesitate this time. "Let's go."

A newspaper sat on the coffee table in front of the shabby couch. Bolan opened it and dropped it over the Beretta. He held the gun in front of him, aimed at Alonzo's stomach. "Don't forget it's here," he warned as he pushed the man out the door and down the stairs.

A ten-year-old Ford LTD sat in the gravel drive on the other side of the garage apartment. Gray primer peeked through the rusty gold on the fenders, and the grille had been smashed and torn halfway off. "Yours?" Bolan asked.

Alonzo nodded.

"You drive."

Bolan took the passenger's seat, keeping the Beretta trained on Alonzo. The dealer backed out of the driveway and headed toward the river side of the city.

Alonzo took him back through the slum area of Asunción. Then the smell of fresh water replaced the barrio's rank odor as they neared the flowing river. They turned along the river, following the thoroughfare north. At the foot of Estrada Unidos, they came upon the small lakes, pleasant waterfalls and gardens that made up Parque Caballero. A mile or two farther on, Alonzo turned into a modern, middle-income residential area.

He looked at Bolan. "Man, I hope he doesn't see this car. He'll recognize it, for sure."

Bolan didn't answer. He watched Alonzo slow and hook a thumb out the window toward a sprawling ranch-style house in the middle of the block. "That's it, man."

The warrior studied the house. It would be easy enough to penetrate, even if there was an alarm system operating.

If Alonzo was telling the truth, and if it was the right house.

"What's the man's name?" the Executioner asked.

"Cantu, man. Pedro Cantu."

"You sure? You wouldn't be lying to me, would you?"

"Hell, no, man!"

"If you're shining me on, you're going to get burned. Go back to the park."

"Huh?"

Bolan shoved the Beretta into his ribs. "Go back to the park."

The battered LTD retraced its route along the riverside, finally pulling back into Parque Caballero. They passed a small lake with a sparkling waterfall, then Bolan ordered Alonzo to the side of the road behind a greenhouse. "Give me the keys and get out."

Alonzo's hand shook as he pulled the keys from the ignition and handed them over. He opened the door, then turned back to Bolan. "Take the car, man, if you need it. Just let me go."

Bolan stepped out of the vehicle and walked around the hood, grabbing Alonzo by the arm and pushing him toward the rear of the LTD. When he reached the trunk, the Executioner inserted the key and popped the lid. "Get in."

"Oh, man . . ." Alonzo whined. "You aren't gonna kill me, are you?"

"Maybe," Bolan replied. "But not right now. If I find out you've lied to me, though, you'll wish you were dead before I'm through."

Alonzo's eyes widened, then his gaze fell to the ground. His lower lip trembled when he spoke. "Look, man," he said. "I . . . I think I might have showed you the wrong house."

"You think?"

"Well, I'm pretty sure. I mean, I showed you the right house, but I could tell by your eyes you were looking at the wrong one . . . I think."

"The ranch house?" Bolan asked.

"Uh, no. The two-story job next to it."

"Right or left?"

"Left, man, left."

Bolan raised the lid higher. "Get in. We'll find out if you're right."

Slowly Alonzo hooked a foot over the bumper and hauled himself into the trunk.

The warrior slammed the lid, then leaned forward. "If I hear any noise out of you, Alonzo, I'll fire a few rounds through the trunk. See what I can hit without looking." He tapped the Beretta on the lid for emphasis, then slid onto the driver's seat.

The sun had begun its descent to the horizon as the Executioner crossed the city limits. Two miles from town, he left the highway, taking a dirt road before cutting across the grassy plains to the grove of trees where he'd landed.

The warrior felt the soft riverside earth under his wheels. It was barely firm enough to keep the big Ford from getting stuck.

He parked the LTD next to the grove of trees. As he got out of the car, he heard the voice in the back. "Where the hell are we, man?"

The Executioner turned, walked back to the trunk and stood next to the fender.

"Hey, man, can't you hear me?" Alonzo rapped lightly on the inside of the lid.

Drawing the Desert Eagle, Bolan aimed high, angling the barrel over where the man would be lying.

Alonzo rapped louder. His voice rose in volume. "Hey, man, you there?"

The dealer was still pounding on the lid as Bolan pulled the trigger. The massive .44 Magnum hollowpoint round echoed across the plains as a gray-edged hole appeared in the trunk lid. The bullet passed harmlessly out the fender and into the grass.

The noise from the trunk suddenly stopped.

The Executioner walked to the trees, pulled the entrenching tool from the dirt and began to dig. Five minutes later he hauled his pack out of the ground and filled the dirt back in over the parachute.

He tossed the pack into the back of the LTD and slid behind the wheel. Alonzo remained silent on the way back to the city. The Executioner pulled the Ford to a halt down the street from the Cantu residence. Cutting the engine, he reached over the seat and pulled a Simmons 25 × 50 spotter's scope from his pack. Focusing the 50 mm lens on the porch in front of the ranch house, he saw the large *R* on the front door. Beneath the letter a gold-plated nameplate read Robles, Armando and Ruth.

Bolan shifted his gaze, readjusting the lens to the two story house on the left. Squinting through the scope, he read the engraved script letters on the mailbox: Cantu, Pedro M.

The Executioner glanced out the window at the sun as it fell wearily over the horizon. He dropped the spotter's scope back into his backpack and started the engine.

It would be dark soon. Time to pay Pedro Cantu a friendly visit.

10

Bolan pulled his backpack over the seat and yanked down the zipper. He dressed quickly, maneuvering his body within the front seat of the LTD as he donned his blacksuit and slid into the Beretta's shoulder rig. Looping a black nylon utility belt around his waist, he added the .44 Magnum Desert Eagle. Shifting the Cold Steel Magnum Tanto knife from the ankle rig to a hard plastic quick-draw sheath, he slid it onto the belt opposite the Eagle.

A handful of the plastic Flex-Cuffs went into one of the pockets of his suit. Digging deeper into the backpack, the warrior came up with a long plastic tube. Twisting the cap, he dulled the skin on his face and hands with black, night-combat cosmetics.

Bolan opened the door and stepped out onto the pavement. The houses of the neighborhood were all dark. A lone streetlight at the end of the block provided the neighborhood's only illumination.

He walked swiftly to the trunk. He hadn't spoken to Alonzo since his "warning" shot earlier, and the man's frightened eyes opened wide as Bolan lifted the lid.

The Executioner rested his hand on the butt of the Desert Eagle. "I want you to keep quiet just a little longer, Alonzo. Be a good boy, and you might live through the night." He paused. "Now, I know what's going through your mind. You can see I'm going someplace and you'll be alone. You figure that as soon as I'm gone, you can yell, scream, bang on the trunk, and someone will hear you, right?"

Alonzo remained silent.

"Well, that's right," Bolan went on. "But keep one thing in mind. You don't know how far away I'll be or when I'll be back. That 'someone' who hears you just might be me. And you know what will happen if it is."

Alonzo nodded, and Bolan slammed the trunk.

The warrior stayed close to the houses along the block, letting the shadows escort him to the two-story dwelling next to the ranch house. When he reached the driveway, he paused in the surrounding shrubs. The side of the house led to a spacious backyard. The windows over the garage appeared to lead to a bedroom. The garage was attached to the house itself by a porched side entrance.

The Executioner stole quietly from the bushes to the porch. He eased open the screen door, then moved across the concrete to the entrance. Eight small windows comprised the top half of the door, and Bolan looked through to see the first flight of a back staircase.

Leaving the porch, Bolan crept by the front of the house, passing grate-covered window wells that indicated a basement below. He looked through a large

picture window and saw a formal dining room. Above
the long oak table, the teardrops of a multicolored
chandelier sparkled in the moonlight that shone
through the open draperies. Tall, thin windows
flanked the front door. Through them, just beyond the
door, the warrior could see the main staircase leading
to the second floor.

Another picture window on the other side of the
front door revealed the living room. The room was
furnished with soft couches and chairs. A white brick
fireplace had been built into a side wall, and the wall
at the far end of the long room was made of glass. On
the other side of the glass, plants, potted trees and a
wrought-iron table and chairs made up the trappings
of a conservatory. Shining through the leaves and
branches from the rear windows, Bolan could see the
backyard lights.

The smaller window at the corner of the house was
dark, the draperies pulled tight. Bolan crept around
the side of the house and came to a screened-in porch.
In the wall opposite the door was the metal box housing the alarm system.

The warrior quickly reconned the rest of the backyard. A curious statue of an eagle sat in the center of
a brick-walled planter, just behind the conservatory.
On the other side of the glass room were the last windows before the rear door to the garage led into the
kitchen.

Returning to the back porch, the Executioner tried
the screen door. Locked.

The Magnum Tanto made quick work of the screen, and Bolan reached through to flip the catch. Moving directly to the alarm housing, he pried the door open with his blade. Inside he found an archaic system of wires running through the box. They evidently linked up to the various doors and windows of the house.

The Executioner cut them all.

The solid oak door to the house had a narrow ledge running horizontally across the center. Just above the ledge, a slim crack split the door in half. The lower section was secured by a strong dead-bolt lock.

Bolan shook his head, wondering who had advised Cantu on his security system. The top half of the door was held to the bottom by nothing more than a flat-bar slip lock, visible through the crack between the two sections.

The warrior slipped his knife through the crack, its razor edge biting lightly into the softer iron. Gripping the blade's rubber handle, he twisted his wrist back and forth, working the bar up and out of its slot.

Pushing the top of the door inward, the Executioner pulled himself up and into the house, then closed the door. He pulled the small Mini Maglite flashlight from a pocket of his blacksuit. The strong beam revealed an informal den area, with comfortable-looking couches and easy chairs. A large-screen television stood against the wall at one end, and at the other was a built-in wet bar.

The Executioner walked quietly, crossing the hardwood floor to another two-section door that led to the conservatory. Killing the flash, he let the moon and the lights from the backyard guide him past the living room, down a short hallway, past a half bath and into the kitchen.

The side porch sat opposite the kitchen. Bolan reached it, then started up the winding back staircase.

On the second floor, he turned right into a converted game room. A pool table was in the middle of the room, surrounded by a variety of video games. The only clue that the area had originally been a bedroom was the bunk beds built into one of the walls.

Bolan stayed near the wall to minimize the creaking sounds as he walked down a long hall. He passed an empty bedroom, then stepped out onto a large upstairs foyer at the top of the main staircase. Circling the rail, he passed another bedroom. An unoccupied, frilly canopy bed stood on the far wall next to the window, bathed in the moonlight shining through the open shades.

The door to the final room was closed. Bolan pressed his ear against the wood and heard soft, feminine breathing. The almost catlike purr was suddenly broken by a loud, shrill snore—male.

The warrior drew the Beretta, eased open the door and slipped inside.

A night-light plugged into the outlet next to the bed reflected off three sleeping faces. On each side of the king-size bed lay a pretty, young, blond-haired woman.

In the middle snored a fat, hairy man.

The Executioner moved swiftly, crossing to the nearer woman and leaning forward to clasp a hand

over her mouth. Her terror-filled eyes opened wide as
Bolan touched the Beretta to her forehead. He leaned
down, whispering into her ear, "Don't scream Do exactly what I tell you, and you won't get hurt."

The woman nodded.

Pedro Cantu's loud, vulgar snoring continued as
Bolan pulled the covers back and helped the nude
woman to her feet. He led her to a couch next to the
front window. Binding both her wrists and ankles with
Flex-Cuffs, he moved to the far side of the bed and
repeated the process with the other woman.

As he looked into the frightened eyes once more, the
Executioner was struck by a sudden déjà vu. The two
were identical twins, he realized as he seated the second woman next to her sister.

Returning to the bed, the Executioner holstered the
Beretta and drew the knife from his belt.

A reading light sat on a shelf in the headboard.
Bolan angled the bulb toward Pedro Cantu's closed
eyes. Pressing the knife into the folds of skin beneath
the fat man's chin, he switched on the light.

Cantu's first reaction was a harsh, resonant burp.
Then his plump eyelids rose back into his head. The
irises shot down, trying vainly to focus on the steel he
could feel against his Adam's apple.

"Time to talk," Bolan told him, "or time to die.
You decide, Cantu."

The man squinted up into the light, trying to see the
face behind it. His voice trembled when he spoke.
"Who the hell are you?"

Bolan pressed lightly on the blade. A thin line of blood appeared beneath the steel and trickled down his prisoner's throat. He raised the blade to the squinting eyes and let a drop fall onto the flabby face. "It's my job to ask the questions. Yours is to provide the answers."

Cantu nodded.

"Who do you work for?"

The drop of blood rolled down Cantu's cheek to his neck. "I'm . . . self-employed," he whispered raspily. "Import-export business that deals in—"

"I don't have time to play games. I'm not talking about whatever front you use. Tell me who's behind your drug operation, or this knife will be applied to your throat with a lot more vigor."

"Rocha. Coapac de la Rocha."

Bolan nodded. Rocha. Kurtzman had suspected the man might be expanding his nickel-and-dime operation. Now it had been confirmed. It made sense. Coapac de la Rocha had grown tired of contracting to the big cartels. He wanted a bigger piece of the action.

"Where's he operate out of?" Bolan demanded.

"He's got offices here in Asunción," Cantu replied.

"I'm talking about coca, friend. If he exports leather goods or lace or llamas, for that matter, I don't care about his front offices, either." He slid the Tanto slowly along Cantu's neck. "Now I'll ask you one more time. Where's his main operation located, the trucks and planes he uses to transport the leaves?"

"Green Hell," Cantu said quickly. "Somewhere in Green Hell. But God, I don't know where. You've got to believe me, I've never been there!"

"Where is he now?"

Cantu shook his head. A bead of sweat dripped from his forehead to his cheek, following the same path the blood had taken through the flabby folds of skin. "I don't know. There's a rumor..."

Bolan prodded him with the knife. "Go on."

"There's a rumor that he's out of the country somewhere, setting up something big."

The warrior frowned. "Where does he stay when he's in Asunción? At his office? Does he have an apartment, a house, what?"

"He's... he's got a girlfriend. I think he stays with her."

"What's her name?"

"I don't know. I swear, I don't know. Rocha doesn't talk about her. I get the feeling..."

Bolan tapped the knife on the man's cheek. "What feeling?"

"I don't know, really. It's almost like he's ashamed of her or something." Cantu took a deep breath. "But don't tell him I said that. I don't know. It's just that I've never seen her with him."

Bolan slid the knife back into his sheath. Pulling more of the Flex-Cuffs from his pocket, he secured Cantu's wrists and ankles, then stood. "Don't go anywhere. I'll be right back."

Descending the main staircase, the Executioner opened the front door and jogged down the block to the LTD. Sliding behind the wheel, he pulled the car into Cantu's driveway, got out and opened the trunk.

"You're gonna kill me," Alonzo whined as Bolan pulled him out. "I know it, man. You're gonna off me right now, ain't you?"

The warrior didn't answer. Pushing Alonzo along with the Beretta, he forced him across the front lawn and into the house.

When they reached the bedroom, Cantu was still squinting against the light. Bolan wrapped more of the plastic cuffs around Alonzo and dropped him on the bed next to Cantu.

When the fat man saw who'd led the big man in black to his house, he snarled, "If this bastard doesn't kill you, Alonzo, I *will*."

"Shut up," Bolan growled, "and listen. Listen real good, because both your lives depend on it. Neither one of you is going to die. At least not from my hand—at least not today."

The strain on both men's faces faded slightly.

"But," the Executioner went on, "that's only because I want you to deliver a message to Rocha. Tell him he's had it good in the coke trade so far. Not much competition. But those days are over." He paused, letting it sink in. "Tell Rocha there's a new kid on the block."

Cantu's eyes widened. "You're not the police? Not DEA?"

"Hell, no, man," Alonzo cut in. "If he is, he broke every damn rule in the book."

Bolan kept his eyes on Cantu. "I'm the competition, friend." He turned to Alonzo. "Your orders are simple. Disappear. If I ever see you again, I'll put a bullet in your brain."

The black man nodded vigorously.

The warrior turned back to Cantu. "You stay in place. Your job is to get more information on the operation.

Don't even think about trying to rabbit on me, Pedro. I found you here, and I'll find you anywhere you try to hide. You understand?"

Pedro Cantu opened his mouth to speak, but the words caught in his throat. Finally he nodded his head.

The house took on a dead, ghostly silence as the Executioner faded out of the room, down the stairs and into the night.

11

In spite of the efforts of the overworked air-conditioning unit, the heat of Green Hell seemed to pour through every crack and crevice in the house.

Seated on one of the couches in the living room, Coapac de la Rocha watched Mario Merito wipe sweat from his brow and smiled inwardly. His own glands had grown accustomed to the sweltering heat. He remained dry, another comforting reminder that they were on his turf. It was his guests who were aliens in a strange land.

The front doorbell chimed, and both Rocha and Merito rose to their feet, watching through the open entrance to the vestibule as Julio hurried to the front door.

The butler ushered in another sweating man in a navy blue pin-striped suit. "I am sorry, Mr. Vivas," Julio said in apology, "but I must..."

The newcomer's lip curled. He shook his head in disgust, then slowly raised his arms over his head.

Julio started at his shoulders, quickly patting him down. The butler turned to Rocha. "He is clean, sir." Looking back to the visitor, he said, "Once again, I am sorry."

Julio walked the man into the living room, then stopped. "Mr. Manuel Vivas," he announced. "Of Medellín."

Rocha bowed slightly and stepped forward with his hand extended. Vivas took it, then Rocha indicated the couch across from the other man. "Please have a seat, Mr. Vivas," he said graciously. "Have you met Mario Merito?" He turned to his other guest.

Merito and Vivas stared defiantly at each other. Neither attempted to shake hands.

Vivas's lip curled again. "We have spoken on the phone," he finally said, then took a seat on the couch.

"Excellent," Rocha said. "Before we begin—"

The words were no sooner out of his mouth than Julio returned to the room carrying a wide silver tray. Napkins, spoons and three elaborately painted porcelain cups with matching saucers circled a stainless-steel coffeepot in the center of the tray. The butler set the tray on the coffee table between Vivas and Merito and disappeared once more.

"As I was about to say," Rocha continued. "before we begin, let us enjoy a cup of Latin America's *second* finest export product—coffee."

The remark brought a thin smile to the lips of Merito. Vivas sat sullenly staring at the overhead fan.

Rocha poured three cups of strong black coffee. "Cream or sugar?" he asked, looking up.

Both men shook their heads.

Rocha passed a cup and saucer to each man, then sat back in his seat. "Then let us begin. As you are both aware, I've been hired to settle a dispute between your two factions. You, Mr. Vivas, represent the oldest and most powerful operation in all of South America—the Medellín cartel.''

Vivas nodded.

"And you, Mr. Merito," Rocha went on, "are here on behalf of the Manaus cartel of Bolivia, a younger— but no less energetic—group of investors."

"Yes."

Rocha looked up at the fan and sighed. "An unfortunate situation has arisen. But I understand the actual location of the dispute is in the United States, rather than here, and it is on the street level of business. The retail level, so to speak?"

Vivas nodded vigorously. "That is correct, Mr. Rocha. In Miami. The Bolivians have invaded territories that have been controlled by us for two decades."

Next to him, Rocha felt Merito stiffen.

Vivas set his coffee cup in the saucer. "They run rampant through the streets like a pack of—"

Rocha held up his hand. "Please. Allow me to try to sum up the situation in a manner that will offend none of us." He turned to Merito. "Mr. Merito, your people have infringed upon the territories that the Medellín cartel has controlled for years. Is this correct?"

A cruel smile flitted across Merito's face. He took a sip of coffee and continued to hold the cup. "I've seen no deed to the streets of Miami, or any other city, in the hands of Mr. Vivas. The money to be made in Miami is for he who takes it." His eyes narrowed. He put his cup down and leaned forward toward Vivas. "It's for he who is strongest."

Rocha placed a hand lightly on Merito's forearm. "Yes, that is the way of the jungle. The way of animals and prehistoric cavemen. But when our ancestors rose to walk on two legs, they also learned another valuable lesson. In order to survive the onslaught of more-ferocious beasts than themselves, cooperation was necessary." He watched Merito's eyes. The Bolivian didn't blink or change expressions. "And it's cooperation I must insist on at this time. It's your ability to cooperate—both of you—that led your superiors to choose you for this meeting." He paused and drew in a deep breath. "And it's my ability to moderate that led them to choose me, and place me in charge, with final power in this matter."

This time it was Vivas's eyes that narrowed. "And for what reason have they delegated you this power? You have no interest in this."

"Not directly," Rocha agreed. "Which is precisely why I can, and will, be impartial." He paused. "I wish to remind you both of something without offending you. Your leaders are well aware that violence between your two factions can lead only to disaster for both cartels. In order to avoid bloodshed, they have agreed to abide by my decision, regardless of what it may be. If they trust me, should you not, as well?"

He leaned forward and lifted a tiny silver bell from the tray. It tinkled lightly in his hand, and a moment later Julio appeared carrying an easel-mounted bulletin board. A large map of Dade County, Florida, had been tacked to the board with pushpins. Thick black lines from a marking pencil had divided the county into sectors.

Rocha rose and took a wooden pointer from Julio. For a moment he felt vaguely foolish, like one of his professors at the university. But he proceeded.

"As I see it," he said, "there are two major areas of Dade County where street-level sales are most lucrative. The downtown area, where large quantities of crack and *suco* are purchased—" he tapped the map in the center "—and Miami Beach, where refined cocaine is still the drug of choice." The pointer moved across Biscayne Bay to the island. "Naturally there is less danger dealing with the wealthier people on the beach. Fewer police interventions, and the people are...cleaner, shall we say? Of course, the dealers you employ at this level are expendable. Basically what I am trying to say is that the beach is more-pleasant work. But the large volume of sales in the downtown area yields a slightly higher overall profit." Dropping the pointer to his side, he turned back to the men.

"Gentlemen, because the Medellín cartel has long been established, Mr. Vivas, you may take your choice between the two major areas. Mr. Merito will have the other. Then we will break the rest of Dade County into districts and divide them equally." He turned to Vivas. "Which will you have? The beach or downtown?"

"We will have both," Vivas snarled. He stared at Rocha, challenging him with his eyes.

"No, Mr. Vivas," Rocha said quietly, "you will have one or the other." He held his breath. The moment of truth was at hand. He would either break the will of this man, or the man would break him. "And if you don't choose quickly, I'll give the decision to Mr. Merito."

With eyes full of hate, Vivas stared back. Finally he said, "We will take the beach."

Rocha nodded. Lifting the marking pencil, he drew lines across the map, dividing the rest of Miami into sectors and writing in the average annual income for each area. Then, coupling each sector with one of similar profit, he divided the town between the two men, giving first one, then the other, his choice.

While he talked, Rocha thought back to his meeting in Taiwan. Soon the day would come when he no longer depended on such trivial things as transporting coca products or settling the petty disputes of men such as Vivas and Merito.

When he had finished, Rocha took his seat and poured more coffee into each man's cup. Settling back on the divan, he said, "And now, gentlemen. I wish you to take a message back to your respective associates." He didn't fight the smile that came to his lips at both Vivas's and Merito's puzzled expressions. "Please inform them that I have arranged for the westward shipment of the drug known as ice. The crack of amphetamines, so to speak. You are both familiar with it?"

Vivas and Merito nodded.

"Good. Inform them that my associates in the Orient are eager to purchase our coca products. There will be great profit in this arrangement for us all."

Rocha rose to his feet, his gaze focused on the shocked looks that had replaced the curiosity. And rightly so. The major cartels in South America had tried unsuccessfully for years to open a worldwide trade. "Gentlemen, we will have the first truly international cartel the world has ever seen." He paused. "The wealth will be shared among us. But please inform your superiors that *I* will be in charge." He watched the staggering news sink in and saw the doubt on the men's faces as each wondered if what he said was true.

Rocha stared back, letting the smile fade from his face. "Participation, of course, will be voluntary. No one will be forced to become part of this multibillion-dollar enterprise. But if they choose to be—" he paused once more for emphasis "—then they will have to deal through me."

Suddenly Julio rushed into the room, breaking the spell. The usually composed butler's eyes were wide with apprehension. "Please pardon my intrusion, sir but I must speak to you immediately."

Rocha felt the anger sweep through his veins. His moment of glory had been shortened by whatever small crisis Julio had encountered. He forced the anger into submission.

There would be many more moments of glory to come.

He followed the butler through the vestibule into the kitchen. Julio shut the door and turned to him. "Sir," he almost whispered, "I have just received a phone call. We have a slight problem."

Rocha felt the anger in his veins disappear completely as Julio went on. And when the butler got to the part about the "new kid on the block," the anger became ice water.

When Julio finished, Rocha lifted the kitchen phone from the wall, punched two buttons and spoke into the receiver. "Pepe, send Ordonez and Domenguin to me immediately. I'll be in the kitchen."

A few moments later two men dressed in light slacks and open-collared sport shirts entered the kitchen from the back door. They stood at attention as Rocha relayed the facts that Julio had given him.

"Find this man in black. Find him tonight and bring me his head." Rocha felt the snarl curl his lip. "Or you might lose yours."

THE STREETLIGHTS LINING both sides of Calle el Paraguay Independiente flickered off and on, as though trying to decide if night had really come. In the twilight the LTD cruised slowly past the government buildings, motels and businesses that ran along the river.

The eyes of the big man behind the wheel scanned the roadway. He had driven along the river all afternoon, waiting patiently for the attack he knew would come.

Bolan listened to the loose front grille rattle as he braked at a stoplight. Driving Alonzo's easily identifiable Ford through the streets of Asunción would have amounted to suicide for most men. To the Executioner, the battered LTD was simply bait.

The light turned green, and the warrior pulled away. Dealing with Coapac de la Rocha had seemed simple at first. Locate the compound—and take him out. The drug lord's operation was somewhere in Green Hell, a particularly dry and bleak section of the Chaco. Three Mennonite colonies raised cattle, cotton and peanuts in the area. Besides those peaceful farmers, the area was practically deserted.

Rocha's drug compound could be found.

But as he'd mulled things over in his mind, Bolan had realized the situation was far more complex than it appeared to be. Locating the compound in Green Hell might take weeks, and Bolan didn't have the time. If what Cantu had said about Rocha setting up a "big deal" was true, the Executioner might not even have days before untold quantities of drugs were flooding the streets of America.

The other obvious battle plan would be to lie in wait in Asunción. If he had offices in the city, Rocha would eventually return. But the operative word was "eventually." Once again it meant time.

Bolan continued down the street, keeping the Ford under the speed limit. Besides the time element, simply taking out Rocha would accomplish little. According to Stony Man, the Incas had taken over the operation from Francisco Juarez, a long-time mobster in the Asunción area. Juarez's syndicate had been small but well organized. Bolan had fought the war on drugs far too long not to know that if Rocha died, someone would step into his shoes—as Rocha himself had done upon Juarez's death. If only the top dog fell to a bullet from the Executioner, the second mutt in line would simply step up and take over.

So the warrior intended to kill the entire pack of mongrels.

Which brought Bolan back to the plan of attack on which he'd finally settled during the wee hours of the morning after leaving Cantu's house. Taking a room at a downtown hotel, his first act had been a call to Hal Brognola. The conversation had been brief but productive.

The Executioner glanced in the direction of the airport, at the darkening sky over the city. It was too early for any of the men he'd requested to arrive, but by now most of them would be in the air.

The members of the DEA Recon and Arrest Team would arrive in Asunción later that night. Deplaning alone or in pairs from flights from all over the two Western continents, they'd be undercover as journalists, businessmen and tourists. As soon as they arrived, Bolan would start to put his plan into operation.

The Executioner was about to enter the cocaine-trafficking business.

Bolan slowed as he neared an intersection. Glancing to his right, he saw a chocolate brown Mercedes stopped under the light at the cross street. Two men wearing open-collared sport shirts stared at the LTD as Bolan cruised through the intersection, their lips moving excitedly behind the windshield.

The warrior passed through the intersection and in the rearview mirror he saw the Mercedes turn and fall in behind.

The "bait" had been spotted.

Bolan continued along the river. The Mercedes followed, letting several cars get between them, staying a hundred yards behind.

As he passed Plaza Constitucione, Bolan glanced at the sun fading over the horizon. Another five minutes, and darkness would fall over the city. Traffic was light, but there were still plenty of witnesses on the road, pedestrians and motorists alike. The men in the Mercedes would realize this, and at the same time know that the same eyes that might distinguish a face or license tag in the twilight wouldn't see as well in the dark. So they would wait. Five minutes would make no difference, so they could afford to avoid unwarranted risks.

The Executioner drove slowly, taking a full ten minutes to cover the four miles to the suburb of Trinidad. Various flora native to the area had been carefully planted along the streets, forming a tunnel of color that led to the botanical and zoological garden.

The garden would have closed for the day by this time, Bolan knew. With any luck there would be no one hanging around the parking lot.

The garden's modern walls of glass and steel glistened under the streetlights flanking the main entrance to the parking lot. Only two cars were there, both rusting old Chevys. As he turned between the lights, Bolan saw a man carrying a mop bucket open the front door and dump water into the flower garden.

The warrior reached down to his side, finding the seat belt and shoulder strap, and snapped them in place. He glanced up into the mirror and watched the Mercedes turn in after him.

A pickup passed by on the street as the Mercedes turned, and in its headlights, the Executioner saw the silhouette of a rifle barrel above the brown car's dashboard.

Bolan drove slowly across the deserted parking lot toward the front entrance. When he reached the middle of the lot, he pressed the accelerator to the floorboard, cutting the wheel hard and skidding into a quick U-turn. He continued to bear down, steering the LTD's screaming tires back toward the oncoming Mercedes. Then, throwing all of his two hundred pounds down onto the brake pedal, he twisted the steering wheel at the last second, letting the LTD glance off the Mercedes's right front fender.

The driver's brow struck the steering wheel, and the head of the man riding shotgun snapped forward, striking the windshield to send a spiderweb pattern shooting through the glass.

Bolan threw the LTD into Park. The Beretta leaped into his hand as he dived through the door and hit the ground. Wild automatic fire from an AK-47 sailed over his head as the man in the passenger's seat recovered. The Executioner rolled to his stomach, the 93-R gripped in both hands.

A 3-round burst sputtered from the suppressed autopistol, the special 147-grain controlled-expansion subsonic 9 mm rounds flattening as they hit the thin metal in the Mercedes's door. Their ragged, deformed configurations drilled into the car, slashing through the flesh of the man riding shotgun.

The AK-47 fell through the window to the parking lot.

The warrior sprang to his feet and raced to the Mercedes, vaulting over the hood to the driver's side. The driver sat dazed, blood pulsing from the contusion above his eyebrows. His only weapon, a Charter Arms Bulldog .44, was still in his belt.

As the stunned man's hand moved toward the gun in slow motion, Bolan reached through the window and pinned his arm to his chest.

Blood continued to gush from the deep wound, pouring over the hardman's face to cover his chin. His crimson-crusted eyebrows rose almost to his hairline as he stared at the Beretta Bolan pointed between his eyes. He looked similar to his partner, who sat next to him gaping wide-eyed at the Mercedes's ceiling. But there was one major difference.

The driver was still breathing.

Bolan stuck his head through the window, his face an inch from the frightened man. "I sent Rocha a message last night. Evidently he misinterpreted it." He pressed the Beretta's suppressor against the driver's face. "The message wasn't an invitation to try to kill me. It was an order to stay out of my way."

The warrior grabbed the driver by the shirt collar and dragged him through the window, dropping him facedown onto the ground. Reaching down, he relieved the man of the .44 and shoved it into his own waistband.

Bolan circled the Mercedes, opened the other door and pulled the dead man out and onto the ground. Walking back to the LTD, he jerked the key from the ignition and flipped it through the air toward the driver. "What's your name?" he asked.

The key fell next to the driver as he rubbed his head along the hairline. "Domenguin."

"I like your car better than mine, Domenguin," Bolan said as he slid behind the wheel of the Mercedes. Twisting the key, he heard the engine roar to life. "A little dented there at the front, and a few bullet holes, but all in all, still better wheels. I'll take it."

The Executioner threw the Mercedes into Drive. "Tell Rocha this isn't the last thing I plan to take away from him." He stepped on the gas and powered out of the parking lot.

12

The Executioner parked the Mercedes down the street from Pedro Cantu's house and killed the engine. He glanced at the luminous hands of his watch—nearly 0200 hours. Quickly scanning the streets and darkened doorways for signs of a trap, he walked back up the street.

Bolan had changed from his blacksuit and now wore black jeans and a matching black shirt. The loose tail fell far below his waist, effectively concealing the Beretta and Desert Eagle that both rode, ready for action, in his belt.

He rang the bell. An eye appeared behind the peephole, then the bolt slid quickly open.

Pedro Cantu had learned a valuable lesson the night before.

It was impossible to hide from the Executioner.

The front door swung open, and Cantu stepped back. The midlevel drug dealer didn't speak as the warrior walked past him.

Bolan stopped at the foot of the staircase and turned back as the door closed behind him. "Are we alone?"

"Yes."

"What did you find out?"

Sweat broke on Cantu's forehead. He glanced nervously around the entryway, then into the living room, as if he might have been wrong—maybe someone had stolen silently into the house during the brief second when he'd opened the door. Finally he looked up into Bolan's eyes. "Rocha has returned."

Bolan knew that. He wouldn't have been attacked so quickly if the drug king was still out of the country.

"He was in Taiwan," Cantu continued, "making a deal with one of the Triads."

The Executioner felt his fists tighten at his sides. For years there had been rumors of alliances between the South American drug cartels and the Asian version of the Mafia, the Chinese Triads. Nothing but cultural differences and distrust had prevented the rumors from becoming fact but now, it appeared that Rocha had overcome those obstacles.

Bolan stepped forward as he spoke. "What else?"

Cantu's feet froze, but his body leaned back awkwardly, away from the big man. "They plan to ship cocaine to the East. Ice to the West," he whispered.

"And?"

"That is all I could learn."

Bolan lifted his shirt and rested his hand on the butt of the Desert Eagle.

"I swear to you, *Señor*," Cantu whined. "It's all I know."

The warrior nodded. "Tell Rocha he can fight my organization if he wants. Or he can deal with us. If he fights, he'll lose. It's that simple." He shoved Cantu out of the way, opened the door and turned back. "By the way. From now on, Cantu, you work for *me*."

"What...what do I do?" Cantu sputtered.

"Keep listening." Then Bolan disappeared into the night once more.

OUTSIDE THE Hotel Excelsior in downtown Asunción, the sun bounced off the mirrored picture window of suite 259 before adding its sparkle to the already dazzling amount of light that surrounded the swimming pool.

Inside the living room of the second-story suite, the one-way mirror was smoked a dark gray, providing a soft view of the tree-encircled pool and courtyard. The decor of the living room was an eclectic yet tasteful hodgepodge of several styles. The sienna silk curtains drawn to the edge of the window matched the pattern woven through the Oriental rug that covered the floor. Landscape prints with brown metal frames covered the "orange-peel" textured walls, which had been painted an even lighter shade of ginger.

The furniture—the end tables, chairs, even the arms and trim on the large couches—was mahogany. In keeping with the earth-tone theme, several wooden sculptures adorned the room. On a table next to one of the couches, two rearing mahogany horses raised a silver-plated salver into the air. On another sat the three "see, hear and speak no evil" monkeys, intricately carved in teak.

A whirlpool, large enough to comfortably accommodate six, sank into the floor against the wall opposite the kitchenette, and just past that a short hall led to three bedrooms. Each had a small half bath and two unusually large closets.

The Executioner stood next to a table in front of the window, his back to the pool. He had no need for elaborate furnishings, and the embellishments of the living room barely registered in the warrior's brain.

He was far more interested in the men seated around the room.

"What we have here," he began, "is a situation in which conventional law enforcement is useless."

A tall, wiry-muscled man wearing blue jeans and a black T-shirt spoke up. "So what else is new?"

Chuckles came from around the room.

Bolan nodded toward the speaker as the man brushed a stray strand of long blond hair behind his ear. "You're right. And that's why you're here."

The rest of the Recon and Arrest Team remained silent as Bolan surveyed them. Pat Elliot, the DEA special agent and the man who'd spoken, was the leader. He sat alone in a wicker love seat, across the room from a large L-shaped couch. Elliot looked as though he could have been Robert Redford's younger, tougher brother. Tall and handsome, he had confidence written across his face in stone.

Seated on the section of the couch closest to Bolan and facing him at a forty-five-degree angle was Dicky Streck. Streck could be called nothing if not "average." He'd been introduced by Elliot as "Anyman" Streck, and Bolan could think of no better nickname to fit the man. Of ordinary height and weight, Streck had medium brown hair that was of medium length. Anyman's face was slightly pudgy, but no more so than that of most men nearing forty. Compared to the other RATs, his clothes were conservative. He wore slightly faded jeans, a slightly faded, short-sleeved, button-down collared shirt, and not-quite-new white cross-trainers.

To Streck's left, Nolan Dow took up the rest of that section of the couch. Dow was of roughly the same height as Anyman, but the resemblance stopped there. He was thin, and thick black chest hair peeked out over the neck of his baggy football jersey. More of the dark hair extended out of the three-quarter sleeves, down his arms, to cover even the backs of his hands.

Two men sat facing Bolan on the other section of the couch—Danny Gober and Mike Davis. Gober wore yellow-lensed shooting glasses. The earpieces disappeared in his straight, shoulder-length hair. He was about six feet tall and powerfully put together, thick shoulders bulging under a ragged denim vest.

But Gober looked small compared to the man who sat next to him. "Frog" Davis, as he'd been introduced to Bolan a moment before, was a massive man who looked like a professional defensive lineman. Curly red hair, bordering on kinky, fired out in random clumps from his huge face. Bulging biceps put the sleeves of his shirt in jeopardy when he bent his elbows, and his chest threatened to rip the buttons off the shirt each time he inhaled.

With the exception of Streck, the four men on the couch all looked to be in their early thirties. They weren't DEA agents. They were the members of the U.S. Army's Special Forces who had been assigned to Elliot. The Green Berets were presently engaged in a different kind of battle—the war on drugs.

Bolan had started to speak again when a knock sounded on the door. Elliot rose and moved across the room with the poise of an athlete. He looked briefly though the peephole, then turned back to the room. "The local boys," he said. "Country attaché." He slid the chain off the door.

Two men in identical lightweight cotton business suits stood in the hallway, and both balanced dollies loaded with wooden crates against their chests. Perspiration dripped from their foreheads. Dark half moons of sweat stained the underarms on their suits as they backed the dollies into the room. They left their cargo upright next to the door.

The taller of the men pulled two key rings from his pocket and handed them to Bolan. He was out of breath when he spoke. "The wheels you ordered." He paused, drawing in air. "They're parked in the west lot. Chevy van and a Lincoln Mark V. Both black. Both new." He led his partner across the room to a set of matching chairs against the wall.

The shorter man's eyes darted quickly over the faces around the room as he followed. Every few seconds his head jerked, quickly twitching either up and down or side to side. It wasn't a severe movement, and the Executioner recognized the symptoms. The man didn't have a simple nervous tic. He had a mild case of Tourette's Syndrome, a nonfatal disease of the central nervous system that caused involuntary muscle contractions.

The Executioner's eyebrows lowered as the men slid into their chairs. "Agents Evans . . . ?" he said.

The taller man raised a hand.

"And Chambers," Bolan finished.

The shorter man turned an up-and-down twitch into a nod.

"Good. I was just about to begin. I'm sure Brognola has briefed you, but let's run over it again. We've got one Coapac de la Rocha, an Inca Indian from Peru who's risen up the ladder of crime in Asunción." Bolan paused and looked toward Evans and Chambers. "You bring a picture?"

Evans reached into a briefcase on the floor next to his chair and came up with an eight-by-ten glossy of a dark-skinned man with narrow eyes and long hair tied back into a ponytail. Hardly of the mug-shot variety, the picture had obviously been taken from concealment with a long-range lens. Rocha was standing on a street corner, talking to a woman who was equally dark complected.

"Rocha calls his organization a 'cartel,'" Bolan went on. "But from what we've gathered so far, it's simply a drug-smuggling mob—with him at the top. But that's right now. Don't make the mistake of underestimating him, gentlemen. If we let him establish this relationship with the Triad, he'll be running the whole cocaine show, not to mention ice. Even now, he's got strong contacts all over the continent. The

Medellín cartel has used him to transport leaves for years.

"So what's our plan of attack, Mr. Belasko?" Streck asked.

Bolan addressed the entire group. "We'll be setting up a phony drug operation. I want Rocha to think that just when he thought he was in the driver's seat, he's got new competition to contend with." He looked from face to face. "I might as well hand out your assignments right now."

A yellow legal pad sat on the table next to Bolan. He leaned down, staring at what he'd written earlier that morning. "Sergeant Gober, you're a pilot?"

"That's correct, sir."

"Then you're in charge of aircraft. I want you to spend the rest of the day around the airport. Hit every legitimate business in the area that sells or leases planes. Get their prices, pick up some brochures, whatever. Just make sure that by the time you're done, everybody in Asunción knows you're looking to buy a whole fleet of aircraft."

The Executioner's gaze rose from the paper, then fell on the enormous man facing him. "You do the same, Frog. But with boats. There's any number of yards along the river. Flash some green. Let word get around that there's another American with big-time cash who's about to go into the shipping business."

The red curls bobbed on Davis's head as he nodded.

"Streck, I want you to find us some office space. Somewhere visible. Downtown. Tell the landlords you represent the North American Research Center. That's a front Brognola has set up in Washington, complete with phony Intel about how it's been used to smuggle guns. If the landlords ask you what we do, tell them research, and that's all they need to know. Get their curiosity going. Let them put two and two together, and realize North American has to be a front. Got it?''

"Affirmative, sir.''

"Elliot,'' Bolan said, "you and Dow will come with me.''

"May I ask what we'll be doing, sir?'' Dow queried.

Bolan felt the grin creep across his face. "Sure. We're going to work on the police-protection end of things.'' He turned to face Evans and Chambers. "Who's the dirtiest cop in Asunción?''

Evans didn't hesitate. "Lieutenant Juan Luis. He runs the 'pad.'''

Bolan nodded. "Okay. Maybe we can do a little housecleaning in that area at the same time we bait the trap for Rocha. Washington's got scant Intel on the men. Anything you two locals might have picked up that hasn't gone through channels yet?''

This time Evans frowned. He leaned forward, resting his head on his fists, and closed his eyes.

Next to him Chambers smiled thinly.

Finally Evans opened his eyes and said, "Word on the street used to be he was gay. No one ever saw him with a woman. Then it leaked out he's got a girl-friend.''

From the corner of his eye, Bolan saw Chambers's head suddenly jerk into a machinegunlike burst of twitches. The thin smile faded, and he glanced nervously at his partner.

"Prostitute is the story," Evans went on. "But he keeps her well hidden if it's true." He stopped talking and looked up at the Executioner.

Bolan continued to look at Evans, but he watched Chambers in his peripheral vision. The man's head jerked harder.

The Executioner controlled the frown he felt forming on his face. He was no doctor, of neurology or anything else. But he'd read a few things about Tourette's Syndrome. While the compulsive muscle contractions were physiologically based, and not brought on by nervousness, stress *did* aggravate the symptoms.

Chambers was obviously under a lot of stress. The Executioner wondered why.

Forcing his mind back to the subject, Bolan thought back to what Cantu had told him about Rocha seeming to be ashamed of his girlfriend. Combined with what Evans had just said, things were beginning to make sense.

Evans spoke again. "Er, Mr. Belasko, none of us know who the hell you really are or who you work for. But we've got our orders, straight from Brognola himself. I'm not questioning your authority. You're in charge, and we'll do whatever you tell us to do." He paused and drew in a deep breath. "But you haven't given Chambers or me anything to do yet."

Bolan smiled. "How long have you been 'in country' here, Evans?"

"Two years."

The warrior looked at Chambers.

"Six months."

With the head twitch, Chambers had probably been marked after his first arrest. Word like that got around drug circles quickly. And as far as Evans was concerned, two years was enough to burn anybody. "You two have a very important assignment," Bolan said. "*Stay away from us.* There's no telling who knows you by now, and being seen with you could jeopardize the whole operation. If you want to help, make sure there's someone by the phone at your office at all times. Someone who can do the 'straight' work we might need done."

Both men nodded.

Bolan grabbed the Magnum Tanto knife from the table next to him and walked to the dollies by the door. Elliot rose without speaking, and they wheeled the wooden crates to the center of the room.

The crates were marked with a bright red logo spelling out Santos Peanuts in flowing cursive letters. Steadying the dolly with his knee, the Executioner used the knife to pry the lid off the top container. He reached in and pulled an M-16 from the oiled paper. Handing it to Elliot, he repeated the process until all five RATs had a weapon.

The next crate contained spare 5.56mm magazines. The one below it was filled with boxes of ammunition.

Turning to the other dolly, Bolan flipped the lid from the box on top. Inside he found jungle fatigues in various sizes and miscellaneous other gear.

The crate below the fatigues yielded a variety of handguns, short-barreled shotguns and knives. The final box contained ammo in various calibers to fit the pistols.

"Pick weapons you can conceal for now," the Executioner ordered them. "We'll leave the rest here. Load up and get on with your assignments. I want everyone to report back here no later than 1800 hours tonight."

Frog Davis stuck a big paw into the pistol box and came up holding a Government Model .45. The big weapon looked like a toy in his hand. He broke open a box of Winchester Silver-Tip .45s and began to feed them into the magazine. Suddenly his head jerked to attention. "It just hit me, Mr. Belasko," he said. "North American Research Center. That's NARC, right?"

Elliot turned to Bolan. A wry grin covered his face. "Don't let the Frog worry you," the RAT team leader said dryly. He turned back to the hulking form with the .45. "He's not real smart, but he can lift heavy things."

The seven warriors laughed, Frog Davis the loudest, as Evans and Chambers said goodbye and left the room.

Bolan watched Chambers take a last nervous look over his shoulder as he closed the door behind him.

The Executioner turned to Elliot. "Who's your best surveillance man?" he asked.

Elliot grinned. "Me. I'm the only cop in the bunch. But Anyman Streck here's not bad . . . for a dogface, anyway. Nobody remembers him from one minute to the next."

"Thanks a hell of a lot."

Bolan turned to Streck, impressed again with how average the man seemed in all ways. As the old FBI saying went, Streck would never stand out in a crowd. "Okay, Anyman," the Executioner said. "Forget looking for offices. Dow can handle that. I want you to get down there and follow Chambers. There's something's not right about him."

"Yeah, no shit," Davis said. He jerked his head up and down.

Elliot's eyes narrowed, and he glared at Davis. "It's a disease, asshole," he growled. "Tourette's Syndrome, and my sister's got it. They can't control it any more than you can quit being so butt-ugly."

Davis's face reddened. "Sorry."

"What Elliot said is true," Bolan said. "But something's making it worse, aggravating it more than usual. That's what concerns me—why?" He turned back to Streck. "Call it a hunch if you want to, but I want you to stake out their office." He found the keys to Rocha's Mercedes in his pocket and handed them to the Green Beret. "Take my vehicle," he said. "They won't recognize it. And if Chambers leaves, especially alone, stick to him like glue."

SETTING UP A MEETING with Paraguayan police lieutenant Juan Luis was a cinch. Graft had to run rampant in Paraguay, because a simple phone call to the man at police headquarters arranged everything. Once again Bolan baited the trap, this time using a lure he knew a man like Luis couldn't resist.

Money.

"I will meet you at one o'clock in the lounge of the Hotel Ita Enramada, Señor Harkin," the lieutenant said, using the alias Bolan had given him. "It is on the river. Do you know it?"

The Executioner remembered passing it the night before. "I'll find it."

"Bueno," the lieutenant said. "Look for a tall, broad-shouldered man with a very thick mustache. That will be me."

"I'll see you there," Bolan said, and hung up.

Pat Elliot came out of one of the bedrooms dressed in a light seersucker suit and carrying a black briefcase in his hand. "You got your transmitter on?" he asked Bolan.

"I'm bugged. I'll take the Lincoln. Follow me in five minutes in the van." He opened the door and left.

A noontime floor show was in progress in the Ita Enramada's lounge when Bolan arrived. He stood in the doorway, letting his eyes adjust to the darkness as he watched twenty topless women in Arabian veils and harem pants dance across the stage.

The Executioner scanned the room. He had only the brief self-description Luis had given him over the phone by which to spot the police lieutenant. As his vision cleared, Bolan saw half a dozen likely candidates.

Then a man of medium height with a pot belly rose from a table in the corner, beckoning. Bolan passed among the tables, heading toward the man.

Tall, broad shouldered, thick mustache.

"Por favor," Luis said, standing up. "Please sit down."

Bolan dropped into the chair across from the man. He noted the elegantly cut silk suit the police lieutenant wore, worth about six months' salary to an honest Paraguayan cop.

"I took the liberty of ordering you a beer. Would you like me to order your meal, as well? I am very familiar with everything on the menu, and it is excellent."

Bolan shook his head. "I didn't come here to eat, Luis. I came to do business."

The man in the silk suit nodded. "Ah, a man who wastes no time. *Bueno.* I like that." He smiled phonily as his head continued to bob. "So what can I do for you, Señor...Harkin, did you say?"

"Yeah. Harkin. That's what I said, I think."

Both men looked up briefly as the wiry, blond Caucasian in the seersucker suit walked in. Taking a seat at a table on the far side of the room, the man set his briefcase nonchalantly on the chair next to him, the end pointing toward Bolan and Luis.

Luis turned back to the Executioner, shooting him a knowing wink. "Of course. What is in a name? So..."

A waitress in a short slit skirt arrived. Luis eyed her lustily as she bent to set their beers on the table.

When she'd left, Bolan said, "I plan to go into business here in Asunción, Lieutenant. I was told you were the man to speak to, that you were a valuable man to have as a contact."

Luis nodded. "*Sí.* I try to help my friends. But before we go on, *Señor* Harkin, I must visit the rest room." He paused. "Would you care to join me?"

Bolan frowned. "No."

Luis chuckled. "I'm afraid you must." He crossed both arms over his chest and patted his ribs several times. "I must check you for wires . . . *bugs,* as you Americans like to call them. At least if we plan to discuss business further."

Bolan took a sip of his beer and stood. "Lead the way."

Across the room, he saw a brief look of concern flash across the face of the man in the seersucker suit. The expression faded quickly.

Good. Elliot was a professional. He wasn't about to blow things because of a slight change in the scenario.

In the men's room, Luis locked the door behind them, then bent to look under the closed doors of the stalls. Turning back to Bolan, he raised his hands. "Please . . ."

Bolan raised his arms.

Smiling, Luis felt quickly around the Executioner's chest, then his waist. His hands halted abruptly over the Beretta and Desert Eagle. Raising Bolan's shirt, the smile widened ear to ear. "They are big ones, yes?"

"They do the job."

Luis patted the Executioner up and down the legs, then stepped back. "You are clean," he pronounced. "Let us return."

At the table once again, Bolan wasted no time. "The organization I represent is called the North American Research Center."

Luis sucked half his beer down in one gulp. "*Sí,* but you are in South America, *señor.*"

Bolan chuckled. "We're branching out."

"Ah, what will you research?"

"Call it artifacts of the ancient Indians... or whatever else you want to. Regardless, we'll be making shipments to the U.S. and Europe... so the artifacts can be studied further. They'll be very valuable. And very... fragile. I am willing to pay to make sure that curious law-enforcement officials don't accidentally destroy them thinking they might be something else. Do you understand?"

Luis nodded. "Would you care to return to the rest room?"

Bolan frowned again. "Why?"

"I thought you might care to check *me* for hidden transmitters. You are talking in circles. Like a man who does not trust me." He waved a hand in front of his face. "Let us call a spade a spade, as you Americans like to say. You are entering the cocaine business, and you would like my protection. Correct?"

"Correct."

"Good, *señor.* You may have it . . . for twenty percent of your profits."

Bolan chuckled and shook his head. "A little steep, amigo," he said. "I'll give you five."

"Fifteen," Luis countered.

"Call it ten, and we have a deal."

The Executioner felt the soft pudgy flesh of Luis's sweaty palm as they shook hands over the table.

"There is a small problem," the policeman said. "I have a friend. Another friend such as yourself. He will not be happy to know you are entering the same business he is in."

"Yes," Bolan said. "Coapac de la Rocha."

"You know him?"

"I've met a few of his friends, but not him. Maybe you could give him a message for me. Tell him the next time one of his goons comes looking for me, it won't just be the goon who ends up in a body bag."

Luis's eyebrows narrowed.

"Tell Rocha I'll take it personally next time, and come looking for *him.* He can't beat us, Lieutenant. If he's smart, he'll deal with us. There's enough for everyone."

Luis shrugged. "Any dispute between the two of you is your business. But I will pass your message on."

Bolan rose and pulled a small white card from his shirt pocket. With a ballpoint pen, he wrote the Excelsior's phone number and his extension. Handing it to Luis, he said, "I'll be in touch," then walked out into the sunshine.

Luis would give the number to Rocha—of that he was certain. which meant a phone call from the drug lord sooner or later.

Half an hour later the Executioner stuck the key in the door of the suite. Inside he dropped to one of the couches and pulled the Beretta from his slacks.

The door opened again, and Elliot walked in. "Got you damn well on video," the RAT leader said, pointing to the tiny window in the end of the briefcase. "How about audio? Scared the piss out of me when he took you to the men's room. I guess he didn't check you for bugs after all."

"Oh, he checked all right. Just not very well." He hit the magazine release on the Beretta, and the clip fell to the couch.

Elliot stepped forward frowning, reached down and picked up the magazine. "Well, I'll be damned." He reached into the stripped box and pulled out the transmitter. "You had it in here?"

Bolan nodded.

"Shit, you got balls bigger than me. I wouldn't even go to the bathroom without a loaded gun these days."

"I hated to myself," the Executioner agreed. He lifted his shirt and tapped the butt of the monstrous Desert Eagle. "That's why I brought this along. It serves pretty well in a pinch."

Elliot's grin spread across his face. He opened the briefcase and removed the video camera. "Well, hell. Even if we don't get anything else accomplished, at least we've made a dirty cop."

Bolan stared up at him. He saw the DEA man's smile disappear as he felt his own face stiffen. "You've never worked with me before, Elliot," he told the RAT team leader. "We haven't even started yet."

13

Josefa Pescadora heard the soft rap outside her room. She glanced at the clock—12:25.

Slipping a short, V-necked nightgown over her head, she hurried to the door. "You're late," she said as she twisted the knob.

Alan Chambers's head twitched up and down. "I know." He held his sport coat over his left arm as he stepped through the door and took her in his arms. "I'm sorry. It's been an unusual day."

Josefa broke free of his embrace. She felt his eyes on her back as she walked to the bed and sat down. Alan hung his coat over her bureau chair and followed. He sat next to her on the bed.

Like a well-trained puppy, she thought.

Alan's head continued to jerk, even worse than usual, Josefa thought. His eyes flickered to the clock on the table. "We won't have time to make love," he said. "I've got to be back on time today."

A thrill swept through Josefa's heart. She would have a day's reprieve from the man's body. But the thrill was quickly replaced with curiosity. An unusual day for a DEA agent meant something big was about to happen. And for someone in her position, the knowledge of something big could be turned into money.

Josefa reached up, massaging the tense muscles in the back of Alan's neck. He closed his eyes. "God, that feels good," he whispered.

She watched the head twitch diminish as he began to relax. "You have had not only an unusual day, my love, you have had an exhausting one, yes?"

"Yes."

Josefa moved her hands down his neck to his shoulders. "Then rest. Relax. Tell Maria your problems. She will make them better."

"We're . . . we're about to move on Rocha, I think. There's a RAT team in from the States. They're being led by this big son of a bitch. Special operative of some kind. Nobody seems to know who the hell he is, but he's in charge. He might be CIA, but somehow I don't think so. He's more like the Green Beanie RATs in a lot of ways. Maybe he's a cop, but he seems more soldier." Alan opened his eyes and turned to Josefa. "By the way, where *is* Rocha?"

"He has returned to Green Hell." She bore down slightly with her fingernails. Alan winced, then closed his eyes again. "So," she said softly, "what do the RATs plan to do?"

Alan took a long time to answer. Finally he said, "It's classified."

Josefa moved her hands lower, massaging the tight muscles of his lower back. He would tell her. He always did. But first he had to pretend that he wouldn't. Remind himself he was an honest, dedicated DEA agent. If he intended to be back at the office by one, he would have to leave in less than ten minutes.

She would have to hurry. But she still had time.

"Alan," Josefa purred, "you are a mass of tension and loose ends. Take off your shirt and lie down on your stomach. I will make you feel better."

Alan did what he was told, lying crosswise across the king-size bed. "I love you," he whispered.

Josefa forced the words to sound sincere. "I love you, too." She straddled his back and began kneading the flesh beneath the skin. She would wait until the right moment before bringing up the RATs again.

Alan's breathing quieted as she worked her way down his back. When she reached his belt, she placed both hands on the back of his upper thigh. "My poor baby," she breathed. "Even your legs are a mass of knots. Take off your pants."

Alan protested only briefly. "But I've got to be back—"

"Shh. You have time. Let *me* worry about that."

Alan obeyed.

Josefa worked her fingers into the backs of his thighs. She saw his neck tighten slightly when her hand moved between his legs. He relaxed again, then moaned softly as Josefa began to rub him gently through his white cotton shorts.

"I love you, Maria," he murmured.

"I love you, too." She squeezed him lightly, studying the back of his neck. The twitch was almost imperceptible now. She leaned forward, whispering into his ear. "If the RATs move on Rocha too quickly," she whispered, "we may not have time to carry out our own plan."

Alan didn't answer. He continued to moan softly. His breath came in short, irregular pants.

"We must act soon," Josefa continued. With her free hand she worked Alan's underwear over his hips, then reached back between his legs, closing her fingers tightly around him and continuing the slow massage.

"God... Maria..."

"We must decide when to act, Alan. What are the RATs planning?"

"I can't... it's classified."

Josefa's hand stopped abruptly. "Alan, don't you trust me?"

He gasped as her hand moved again. "Setting up... a phony smuggling op..." he said between breaths. "Going to make Rocha think... oh, God, Maria... make him think there's competition... flush him out..."

Hidden behind him, Josefa smiled. Her hand increased speed. That information would be invaluable to Rocha. But she would have to carefully weigh the odds. If she decided Alan Chambers had the balls to carry through with her plan, it would be far more profitable to keep the information to herself. But if not...

Josefa's stomach soured in disgust at Alan's weakness. She pumped harder with her hand, determined to end his pleasure quickly, now that she had what she wanted. She would have to decide which path to take.

If Alan proved willing, she would leave Asunción with a million dollars. If not, at least she would have whatever Rocha paid her for the information about the RATs.

Considerably less than a million, no doubt. But better than nothing.

Alan's body suddenly stiffened. A low, guttural groan escaped his lips. He jerked spasmodically several times, then fell forward, burying his face in the sheets.

Josefa stared at the back of his head in revulsion. At least the nauseating twitch was gone.

Josefa removed her hand and leaned forward, kissing him on the back of the neck. "It is time for you to go, Alan," she whispered softly.

Alan turned over and sat up. He pulled his underwear up to his waist and reached for his trousers on the bedpost.

"We must act quickly," Josefa reminded him.

He stood, stepping into his slacks, and looked down at her. His face was red. Whether it came from lust, embarrassment, anger or stress, Josefa couldn't be certain. What she could be certain of was the confusion in his eyes. "I . . . I don't know, Maria."

"But it's a good plan, Alan. It's simple. That's why it will work."

Alan began to button his shirt. "Yes. It would work. But it's just that—"

"Do you want me, Alan?"

"You know I do."

"Then you will have me. And we'll leave Asunción. Leave all of South America if you wish. We'll be rich, Alan. You'll never need to worry about money again." She stopped and drew in a deep breath, knowing it deepened the cleavage under her nightgown. "And you'll never have to worry about love, Alan. But first you must do this small thing that I have asked of you."

Alan stared at her as he finished with his shirt. "I want to," he said. "It's just that it goes against everything I've ever believed in. Everything I've been taught. I—"

Josefa felt the rage engulf her body. She tried to hold it in, but a good deal of the fury leaked out in her voice. "You Americans," she said, almost spitting. "With your shallow ideals. You pay lip service to whatever is fashionable at the moment. Right now it is the so-called war on drugs."

Catching herself, Josefa forced her voice to soften. "Lover," she whispered, "don't you understand? Don't you see? If we take Rocha's money, we will *destroy* him. He'll be shamed in front of all the cartels and now even the Triad. He will never import drugs into your country again."

"But we're not just planning to take his money, Josefa. We're planning to take his dope, then sell it for the money. Kill the pilot and the rest of the guards. Murder them, Maria!"

Josefa shook her head. "You still don't understand, do you? Yes, we'll take his cocaine and sell it. But how much difference will that make? If I don't escort the cocaine and ice to America, Rocha will simply send someone else. One way or another, the drugs are destined for the United States. And as far as this murdering that seems to upset you so, how many times have you told me that those who push drugs should be executed? How many times?''

"I don't know."

"So which is better, my love? To deliver the cocaine ourselves on a one-time mission that will destroy Rocha and allow us to disappear and live together in our love? Or let Rocha do it and use the money to finance even more of his deadly trade?''

Alan knotted his tie. He shrugged. "I don't know. I just don't know."

Josefa let her voice take on a vague, threatening edge. "Well, you had better decide soon. Because if you aren't willing to help the woman you love, there are other men who will."

Fear entered Alan's eyes as if he'd seen a ghost. His Adam's apple bobbed up and down as he swallowed. "All right. Set it up. I'll do it."

Josefa Pescadora smiled as he left the room.

DICKY STRECK WAS the last to return to the suite for the meeting that night.

Bolan stared through the peephole before opening the door. It took him a moment to recognize the man. Half of Streck's face was hidden behind black wraparound sunglasses, and sometime since the meeting that morning, Streck had shaved his mustache, the closest thing to a distinguishing feature the RAT had.

The warrior ushered him into the room toward one of the couches, where Streck took a seat.

Briefly Bolan ran down what had happened with Lieutenant Luis. "If he hasn't gotten to Rocha already, it has to be because every telephone in Asunción is out of order. By now our drug-dealing friend will know that it's not just one man causing his problems. There's a whole new group moving in on his territory."

"It won't just be crooked cops stinging his ears," Danny Gober said. He brushed his long hair back over his ears and smiled behind the yellow shooting glasses. "I got a few raised eyebrows around the airport."

"Hell, I'd guess so," Frog Davis boomed. "You should of seen the way the salesmen acted when they saw how many boats I was interested in. And what size. They didn't know whether to fall all over themselves trying to get the commission or head for the nearest pay phone. Man, this Rocha guy must have the whole city in his back pocket."

Bolan nodded. "How about you, Dow? How'd you do with the offices?"

Dow raised a hairy arm and scratched his chest. "Fine," he said. "I must have hit every vacancy in downtown Asunción. I got my share of curious looks, too."

The Executioner turned to Streck. "So. You find out anything of interest on Chambers?"

Streck unwrapped the sunglasses from his forehead. He looked down at the floor as he spoke. "Yeah, but I don't think it's too good."

"Go on," Bolan prompted.

"Well, I got down to the parking lot in time to see Chambers and Evans pull out of the lot. Chambers was driving. I followed them awhile, through the traffic, and all the time I'm worried about them recognizing me if I get too close. I mean, I know I'm the Anyman, but they'd just been here at the meeting and all. I found these shades above the visor. And I'd spotted your equipment pack in the backseat, so I dug through it and found your shaving kit while I drove. That's when I lost the mustache. But then I lost them in traffic. So I drove like a bat out of hell toward the DEA office, and got there just in time to see Chambers let Evans out. He drove off by himself." Streck paused for air.

"And?"

"And now it was Chambers driving like there's a fire at his mama's," Streck went on. "I figure wherever the hell he's going, he just can't wait to get there." He chuckled softly. "Anyway, he pulled up to this old mansionlike place downtown. I pulled in behind him. I had to pray he wouldn't remember me without the face hair. Anyway, he didn't. Besides, the way he was acting, I think he had only one thing on his mind."

"Pussy?" Davis wondered.

"Damn straight. Turns out the old mansion's a high-rollin' whorehouse. I gave Chambers a few seconds, then followed him up the front steps. A couple of other guys were coming out, and he didn't pay them or me any attention. I mean, it's not the type of place where you advertise who you are."

Bolan listened. In the back of his mind, scattered bits of information were fighting to come together.

"So we go into this waiting area which is like an old nineteenth-century living room or something. But instead of mixing with the girls downstairs in the garter belts, Chambers walks right up the stairs to the second floor. Like he owns the damn place." Streck paused again and drew a deep breath. "So I followed him up. Nobody paid either of us any attention. I stopped on the landing and saw him go down the hall into one of the rooms."

"You have a hard-on by then?" Davis asked.

"Hell, yes," Streck said. "You're the only impotent bastard in this outfit." The men laughed and Streck went on. "I walked down the hall real quiet. So I could listen at the door. I mean, I figure if anyone comes out of one of the rooms and catches me, they'll just think I'm some pervert who gets off listening, right?"

"You mean you're not?" Davis said. The five RATs burst out laughing.

"Okay," Streck said when they'd quieted down. "I'm standing there for about five minutes and it's hard—"

"I *bet* it is," Davis said.

"It's hard to *hear*," Streck continued through the RATs' mild hysterics. "But my Spanish isn't so great to begin with, and under the circumstances, I only made out one word that really caught my attention. Then the door to the next room opened and this gal in one of those teddy things walked out."

"And then what?" Davis wanted to know.

Streck's ears colored slightly. "Uh, well, I got laid. Pretty cheap, too."

Bolan waited until the pandemonium quieted. He walked over to where Streck sat on the couch. "The word that caught your attention. What was it?"

"Rocha."

The silence of a graveyard fell over the suite.

Bolan stood there, watching the men. Why would Chambers be talking about Rocha to a prostitute? There were several possibilities. Rocha might own the brothel. He might be a frequent visitor. Or the Asunción crime boss might simply have come up in conversation—he was obviously a well-known figure around town. The whole thing could be perfectly innocent.

But the Executioner's gut instincts didn't tell him that. And there was a darker possibility. Far darker, with grave consequences.

Chambers could be on Rocha's payroll, passing information to the drug king through this prostitute.

If he was, Rocha might have already been tipped to the RATs and to the Executioner's plan.

"What the hell does that mean?" Dow asked.

Bolan didn't answer. He turned and walked to the end table by Davis. Lifting the receiver from the phone, he tapped in the numbers of the DEA's Asunción office.

When the female voice on the other end answered, Bolan said, "Alan Chambers, please." A few seconds later the man was on the line. "Chambers,"

Bolan told him. "Something's come up. We need your help."

"Certainly, Mr. Belasko," came the voice on the other end of the line. "You need me to bring Evans?"

"No. It's not that big a deal. No point in tying up more men than we need. Just come by yourself. What'll it take you, thirty minutes?"

"I'll be there, sir," Chambers said, and hung up.

The warrior dropped the receiver back into the cradle and turned to the RATs.

"To answer your question, Dow," he said. "I don't know what it means."

The Executioner felt his jaw muscles clamp down. "But I intend to find out."

BOLAN STOOD next to the window. In the courtyard below, two pretty teenage girls in skimpy bikinis lay on towels. On the other side of the pool, a pair of boys sat in deck chairs. They whispered back and forth as they studied the girls, trying to decide when and how to make their moves.

In the parking lot to the side of the pool, the warrior saw a dark green Chevy sporting multiple antennae pull into a vacant spot. Alan Chambers exited the vehicle.

Bolan watched him walk toward the hotel. Dirty police officers were more criminal than cop in the Executioner's book. The minute they stepped over the line, they were no better than the thieves and drug pushers they had put behind bars. Maybe they were worse.

But he also knew there was at least one distinct difference between the professional criminal and the majority of dishonest cops.

Dirty cops still believed in right and wrong. They still had consciences and usually regretted what they'd done.

Chambers reached the hotel entrance. "He's here," Bolan announced, turning away from the window. "Elliot, you stay. The rest of you men—" he glanced from Gober and Dow on one couch to Streck and Davis on the other "—make yourselves scarce."

The four Green Beret RATs rose and disappeared down the hall to the bedrooms.

Bolan turned back to the window.

A few minutes later the knock came in the hall. Elliot glanced through the hole, then swung the door open.

Alan Chambers walked in.

Without turning around, Bolan said, "Grab a chair, Chambers."

He heard the rustle of clothes behind him as the man sat on the couch.

"Anybody want a drink?" Elliot's voice came from the kitchenette.

"Sure," Chambers replied. "Scotch, if you've got it."

"Belasko?" Elliot's voice again.

"Nothing."

The Executioner continued to stare out the window as he heard Elliot pouring Chambers's drink. In the reflection from the glass, he saw the RAT leader walk back into the living room and hand Chambers a glass. Elliot dropped into a chair across from the L-shaped couch.

"What can I do for you, Mr. Belasko?" Chambers asked.

Bolan turned around as Chambers raised his glass. There was no point beating around the bush. "You can tell me about the woman you went to see after you left here this morning."

The glass froze halfway to the agent's lips. His head twitched violently up and down. "What woman?"

The warrior walked forward, stopped in front of Chambers and stared down into guilty eyes. "We don't have time to play games."

Slowly Chambers placed the glass on the end table next to him. He leaned forward over his knees and buried his face in his hands. "How did you know?"

"That's not important. What is important is that we evaluate the extent of the damage you've done. Now start at the beginning and tell me the whole story. Now."

Chambers sat back. His eyes were bloodshot, and moisture had formed in the corners. "I'm in love with her, Belasko."

"Oh, shit," Elliot muttered under his breath. He turned his face toward the window.

Bolan didn't answer. He took a seat on the other section of the couch.

Chambers stared vacantly at the ceiling as his head jerked back and forth. "Her name's Maria. I met her with Steve Kapka about six months ago. Kapka was the agent that got it with the MAC-11 on the streets last week. Maria had been his informant for over a year." He stopped, wiped a tear from his face and returned his gaze to Bolan. "I fell in love with her, Belasko. I couldn't help it. She was...*is,* so...we were—"

"You can spare us the details of the courtship," Bolan said. "Let's cut to the chase."

Chambers nodded. "Rocha...visits her. He's in love with her, too." The DEA man looked nervously down at his feet. "But she's in love with *me.* And she passes some damn good information my way about Rocha's operation."

"Give me an example," Bolan demanded.

Chambers nodded eagerly. "Okay, for example, I knew about the Triad connection a long time before anyone else found out."

Bolan stared at him. "Then why didn't you pass it on?"

Chambers face stiffened as he realized he'd backed himself into a corner. Then suddenly he leaned forward again and burst into tears. "I...couldn't."

The Executioner gave him time to get control of himself, then asked, "Why not?"

"It's over. I know that. I might as well come clean." He paused to wipe his face with the back of his sleeve. "She...*we* had a plan. Rocha was going to have her escort the first shipment of coke and ice to the U.S. He was going to pay her a commission. It would have been a million dollars." He looked down at his shoes.

"But that wasn't enough for her. She wanted it all. All ten million."

Bolan put the rest of it together himself. "So with her help, you were going to hijack the load somewhere along the line, right?"

Chambers nodded. "As soon as they got to Florida," he said.

"Kill the guards, take the dope and run away to wonderland with the girl of your dreams," Bolan finished for him. "Is that about it?"

The agent looked pleadingly into the Executioner's eyes. "We were going to get married. And she convinced me it wasn't really so wrong. No matter what we did, Rocha would have gotten the dope to the U.S. But if we stole it, it'd put Rocha out of business for good. It would be his last job. He couldn't ever again—"

"I don't want to hear it," Bolan interrupted. He felt the anger build up in his chest. It was the typical rationalization of a man looking for a reason to do what he wanted to do rather than what was right. "Did it ever occur to you that you had another option? There was another way to stop Rocha."

Chambers stared blankly at him. "What?"

Bolan stood. "You could have done your job. With her help, you could have busted Rocha and put an end to things before the drugs left Asunción."

The agent dropped his gaze back to his shoes. There was a long silence. Then he whispered, "She knows that this is a phony operation you're setting up."

Bolan fought the urge to knock the man unconscious. "I won't bother to ask you how she knows that. Did it ever occur to you that she just might be running the same scam on you that *you* think she is on Rocha?"

"She wouldn't do that. She loves me, Belasko."

Elliot broke in. "Oh, fine, she loves you." Shaking his head in disgust, he went on. "You stupid son of a bitch. How do you think Rocha got word that Craig Waken's team was staked out in Arizona? I'll *tell* you how. The bitch gave Kapka the info on the plane and where it'd be landing. Kapka paid her for it. Then she turned around and told Rocha that a DEA agent who was one of her tricks had let it slip that they knew all about the shipment and were setting up on the site. And that fool paid her, too, because like you, Rocha must start thinking through his pecker every time the bitch takes off her clothes."

Bolan nodded. "You've been a fool, Chambers."

"What's going to happen to me?" he whimpered.

"That's for your superiors to decide," the warrior replied. "I suppose it's not as bad as if you were on Rocha's payroll. Being a total jackass falls somewhere below dishonesty. But the damage is the same."

Elliot's fists rolled into tight balls of fury.

Bolan watched the RAT leader's enraged face. Ninety-nine-point-nine percent of all DEA agents were honest, hardworking men, the Executioner knew, and they had no patience with the other tenth of a percent who made the whole Administration look bad.

"What ought to happen," Elliot said through clenched teeth, "is that we ought to kill you."

Bolan watched Chambers's face twist into a mask of fear.

"But we won't," Bolan said. "We'll see if we can use this mess to our advantage somehow." He stepped in front of Chambers and leaned down, his face an inch away from the terrified man. "But let me tell you something. Listen and listen good. From here on in, you'll follow my orders to the T. Like Elliot told you, you'll do your thinking with your head instead of your crotch. You understand me?"

Chambers's voice cracked when he spoke. "Yes, sir."

"Because what I said about not killing you wasn't a promise by any means. You screw anything up— anything—and I just might change my mind."

Bolan straightened up. "Elliot, stay here. Don't let lover boy out of your sight." He started for the door.

Elliot nodded. He walked to Chambers and pulled the Glock 17 from the weeping agent's holster. "Where you going?" he asked.

The Executioner turned back. "To stop Chambers's girlfriend from getting to Rocha." He opened the door and stared back at Alan Chambers. "If she hasn't already."

He was halfway out the door when the phone rang.

COAPAC DE LA ROCHA FIRED the last round from the Detonics Scoremaster and felt the slide lock open in his hand. He squinted in the sunlight at the black silhouette target at the end of the range.

All eight rounds had gone into the kill zone. Two had found their way to the X-ring.

Rocha stood silently for a moment. "The next magazine shots I fire will do the same to the bastard's heart," he vowed under his breath.

The Asunción crime boss turned from the range and walked past the barracks to the house. Mounting the front steps, he entered the living room, then walked down the hall to his den. He took a seat in one of the thick leather chairs and stared at the bookcases lining the walls. Reaching in his pocket, he produced the small white card.

It was the only link he had to the man he knew he must kill.

Both the phones at his city offices and the Green Hell compound had been ringing off the walls all day. Rocha had heard from a dozen sources that the bastard who'd been giving him migraines had now been joined by several confederates. The men had been all over Asunción, leasing office space, airplanes and boats.

They planned to go into business. That was clear.

Rocha continued to stare at the card, as if it might somehow answer his problems for him. He knew from Lieutenant Luis that the number belonged to the Hotel Excelsior, and the extension would be the same as the room number.

Which meant all he had to do was send a lot of men with machine guns to the room. So many men that this big bastard and his friends would have no chance.

Except for one small complication.

First the Triad representatives had arrived a few hours earlier. Even now Cheung and Ling were napping in two of the guest rooms. They had brought with them a large quantity of ice. In return, the Chinese would receive a combination of refined cocaine and coca paste to take back to Taiwan.

But not for two more days. First the Orientals wanted to see Asunción.

Rocha pulled a long thin cigar from the leather-covered humidor on the table next to him. He picked up a heavy marble lighter and held the end of the cigar just above the flame, rolling it slowly until the edges of the tip glowed in a uniform, orange ring. Sticking the cigar in his mouth, he stared at the card once more.

One of the Triad's biggest reservations about joining forces with the South American cartels had been the violent image portrayed in South America. Not that the Triads were opposed to violence—far from it. Like the mafia in the United States, if it became necessary, they would impose fast and strict punishment on those who dared to cross them. But that rarely became necessary. They had progressed to the point where they ruled through the threat of violence more often than actual violence itself.

They considered any organization that hadn't yet established that luxury to be beneath them, and a threat to the security their respectable images provided.

Rocha inhaled a lungful of smoke and let it drift out his nostrils. The presence of the Triad representatives meant he couldn't just turn the Hotel Excelsior into a shooting gallery. He would lose face.

Rocha dropped the cigar into the ashtray next to the lighter. He stood up and walked to the bookcase against the far wall. Pressing in on the third book from the left on the top shelf, he stepped back. The case rotated slowly outward, revealing a small closet. The Asunción crime boss stepped over a trapdoor in the floor and moved to a shelf in the closet wall. Lifting the top box of .45 hard-nose ammunition from the stack, he pressed the book on his way back to the chair, and the bookcase swung back in place.

He dropped the stainless-steel magazine from the Scoremaster and began to load it. For the moment his hands were tied. He would have to play along, find out what this group calling themselves the North American Research Center had in mind when they said there was enough for everyone.

And then, as soon as Cheung and Ling were on their way back to Taiwan, the usurpers would be dealt with as they deserved.

Rocha finished loading the Scoremaster, shoved the magazine up the butt and placed the weapon on the table. Staring once more at the card, he reached for the phone and tapped the number into the face of the instrument.

"Hotel Excelsior," said a soft feminine voice. "How may I help you?"

"Suite 259."

A moment later he heard the ring, and then someone answered, "Hello?"

"I am Coapac de la Rocha," he announced, waiting for the response.

"So?"

Rocha was taken back. "So," he said uncertainly, "what do I call you?"

"Harkin will do."

"So what do you want, Señor Harkin?"

The low voice on the other end chuckled. "It's not what I want of you, amigo. It's what you need of me—my cooperation."

Blood throbbed in Rocha's temples. His fingers clamped furiously around the phone. He glanced down the hall toward the bedrooms and forced himself to calm down. "Go on."

"You've had a good thing going on down here. My associates and I just want to get in on it. You can live with us, or we can live without you. The choice is yours."

Rocha fought the desire to scream at the man on the other end of the line. Who did the bastard think he was? Coapac de la Rocha could have the American's testicles floating in a jar next to his bed by morning.

A soft snore came down the hall. Rocha glanced again toward Cheung's and Ling's bedrooms. His grip tightened on the receiver.

Just as soon as the Taiwanese were gone, that's exactly what he'd do. He'd cut off the man's balls and stuff them down his throat. Then watch while he bled to death.

"I'm proposing a trade," Harkin said.

"Oh? And what could you possibly have that would interest me?"

"Guns, primarily. That's what we've been into so far. But we're diversifying. We plan to enter the coke trade, as well."

"My men *have* guns," Rocha replied. "You should keep that in mind."

Harkin chuckled. "Smooth, Rocha. Very smooth." The voice grew colder. "But it doesn't impress me. You can always use more firepower, and we need a drug connection."

"Why should I trust you?"

"Because you have no choice. Not if you want to stay in business. Look, Rocha, we know about your new deal with the Triad."

Rocha was too stunned to answer.

"Don't worry," the voice went on. "We don't want all of your action. Just a piece of it. Considering how much money you'll be making, you won't even miss our cut."

The drug lord's hand trembled in fury around the phone. He felt impotent. He had no intention of cutting these newcomers in on the action. But until Cheung and Ling were safely tucked away back in Taiwan, there was nothing he could do.

Rocha cleared his throat. He forced his voice to remain calm. "You have nothing that interests me, Mr. Harkin."

"Sure I do. I propose a trade. Guns for dope. It'll be an act to show good faith on both our parts."

"No. And now I am very busy at the moment. I have important house guests. So if you will excuse me..." Rocha hung up and sat back against the cool leather chair, staring at the ceiling. The blood within his head continued to pound against his skull. He felt the hatred rise up in his chest.

He closed his eyes, forcing himself to breathe steadily, and pictured Josefa in a white wedding dress.

A grin spread across his face. As soon as Cheung and Ling were gone, he would contact Harkin again. If this man wanted to trade guns for cocaine, fine. Rocha would set up a deal to go down in Green Hell, and when the men from the North American Research Center arrived, they would be mowed down by machine guns.

The grin on Rocha's face widened. His head quit pounding and his chest relaxed. He pictured Josefa again. When this was over, if she still insisted, he would let her go to the U.S. with the first shipment of ice. But first he would do his best to convince her it was unnecessary. He would give her the million dollars, as he'd promised before. In either case, he would marry her.

The hatred in Rocha's heart faded away. The pounding in his head disappeared. At long last he would have the woman he loved.

14

Josefa Pescadora poured sangria from the pitcher into a glass. She took a sip and set the glass back down on her bureau. Lifting the hairbrush, she stared at her nude body in the mirror. Her breasts wiggled slightly as she began to brush her hair.

At thirty, she still had her figure. And only a few crow's-feet could be seen at the corners of her eyes. By combining her God-given beauty with the sexual skills she'd mastered over the years, she had become the most sought-after girl in the brothel. And that combination had always gotten her whatever she wanted out of her men.

Josefa stared at her reflection, squinting at the tiny crow's-feet. Were they deeper than she imagined? She watched her breasts wobble with each stroke of the brush. Had they begun to sag, if only the slightest bit?

She set the brush down and continued to stare into the mirror. What would she look like in another ten years, particularly if she continued to lead the kind of life she had for the past ten?

Josefa lifted the glass of sangria to her lips, her eyes never leaving the mirror. A drop of the sweet red wine ran down the corner of her mouth, and she licked it away with her tongue. She had no intention of spending the next ten years as she had the last. There was a big score in her future; she could feel it in her blood.

She would find a man so foolish that he confused lust with trust.

For over a year she had thought that man would be Steve Kapka. But Kapka hadn't been as taken by her charms as she'd imagined. While he had never refused her bed, he had immediately refused her plan. That refusal had cost him his life.

Josefa smiled wickedly into the mirror. May he rot in hell.

Then she had been certain that Alan Chambers would be her ticket to wealth. He was so much weaker than Kapka had been. He had never been able to refuse her anything.

But that had become the problem in itself. Alan was too weak to refuse her, but he might also be too weak to go through with it.

She had worried all afternoon about Alan. His frailties were almost unbearable. When it came time to go through with the plan, could he really do it? Did he have what it would take to shoot the guards Rocha would send with the shipment? Could he murder four or five men—even drug dealers—in cold blood? And then could he bring himself to violate his principles by selling the cocaine and ice himself?

The more she thought about it, the less she believed he could.

Total contempt for the DEA agent flowed through her veins. She stood and walked to the closet. She hated Alan Chambers, hated his feebleness and the cowardly behavior he tried to mask as morality. Most of all, she hated the love he obviously had for her. And, oh God, that maddening way his head bobbed around! Like a balloon filled with helium on the end of a stick. It was irritating enough when he was under no stress, but put the least amount of pressure on the man and his head shimmied and shook as if it might suddenly fly from his neck. How many times had she wanted to grab that head and hold it still? How many times had she wanted to take a shotgun and blow it from his shoulders?

Josefa sorted through the hangers until she found the short Oriental robe. She threw it over her naked shoulders. Someone had given her the robe. Who had it been? Not Rocha. Ah, yes, Martinez. The fat bastard had brought it back to her the time he'd taken his wife and children to Japan.

Josefa sat down on the bed. She felt the tense muscles in her face curl down into a frown and fought against it, knowing it would only hasten the wrinkles. She looked at the phone and thought of Alan again. No. He could never pull it off. He was simply too weak. And she must not let the fear that her beauty was fading push her into a foolish move. There would be another chance.

Sighing, the woman made her decision. She would abort the plan with Alan Chambers. She would call Rocha and pass on the information about the phony drug syndicate the DEA was setting up. Then she would let Rocha talk her into taking the million dollars without "working for it." The money could be put away for emergencies. Somewhere during all of this, she would expose Alan Chambers as a DEA agent, and make sure he met a fate similar to Steve Kapka's.

But she would stall Rocha about leaving the brothel and living with him. Somewhere down the line, there would be another drug shipment to escort. And somewhere down the line, she would meet another DEA agent who would fall for her charms.

A small grin replaced the frown on Josefa's face. What name had Alan mentioned the other day? Ah, yes. Evans.

Josefa rose, walked back to her bureau and pulled a black leather address book from the bottom drawer. She found Rocha's name, then looked for the number next to the words "Green Hell."

Returning to the bed, she set the book down next to her and reached for the phone.

The sudden ring made her hand jerk back. She took a deep breath, then lifted the receiver. "Yes?"

"There is a gentleman here asking for you. Do you know a Mr. Harkin?"

"No."

"He says you were recommended by a man he works with. Someone you are very close to."

"What is his friend's first name?"

There was a brief pause. "Alan."

Josefa hesitated. It made no sense. Alan would never recommend her—to anyone. He wanted her for himself, and like Rocha, it drove him crazy to think about her with other men. But he was so weak—he felt such frustration and guilt. It would be just like him to need someone he could confide in, someone to whom he would be unable to resist telling of his lover's sexual prowess.

A "friend" who might want a taste of that prowess for himself.

"Shall I send him away?"

Josefa thought of Rocha. There was no rush. And until she actually had the million, she could always use the money this man would be willing to spend. "No, send him up."

Josefa replaced the phone and straightened her robe. A moment later she answered the knock at the door.

She was pleasantly surprised at what she saw. The man was big. Handsome in a rough sort of way. He looked almost like some medieval warrior with his chiseled features and broad shoulders.

She hadn't felt anything for a man in a long time. She didn't expect to this time, either. But there was always the chance. And his muscular body *was* appealing.

Josefa opened the door wider, and he entered her room.

She caught herself smiling as she shut the door and unfastened the robe, letting it fall open before she turned around. She stared up into the hard, expressionless face, then slipped her arms up around the man's neck. "And what do you want of me?" she breathed.

The man didn't answer.

Josefa stood on her toes, pressing her open lips against those of the tall man.

He didn't respond.

Josefa pulled back and looked uncertainly into his eyes. "What do you want?" she repeated.

"I'd like you to make a phone call."

It was then that she felt the hard object pressing into her ribs. Looking down, her eyes fell on the biggest gun she'd ever seen.

The man kept the gun aimed at her as he backed toward the closet. Yanking a dress from one of the hangers, he tossed it to her. "Get dressed. We're going for a ride."

BOLAN UNLOCKED THE DOOR to suite 259 and pushed Josefa Pescadora into the living room. Elliot and the rest of the RATs all sat on the L-shaped couch.

Chambers, his eyes still red, sat next to Frog Davis. The confused DEA agent had removed his sport coat. His shirt was soaked with sweat, and the empty holster still rode on his belt. His head twitched wildly when he saw Bolan and Josefa.

"Maria—" he started to say.

Frog Davis elbowed him in the ribs. "Shut up."

Gripping the woman's arm, Bolan guided her to the couch next to Elliot. The RAT leader had both his own Glock 17 and Chambers's jammed into the waistband of his jeans.

When the woman was seated, Bolan lifted the phone. "Call Rocha."

Josefa smiled up at him. "What should I tell him?" she purred seductively. "That I have been kidnapped by a group of handsome, sexy men?"

"That approach won't work for you this time," Bolan told her coldly. "Just tell him you've been kidnapped. That'll be enough. And lady—" the Executioner leaned down, close to her face "—you'd better make it convincing."

The sly smile left Josefa's face as she tapped the buttons. A moment later she spoke into the mouthpiece in Spanish. "It's Josefa."

Across the room, Alan Chambers's head shot up in a furious series of jerks. "*Josefa?* Maria, what—"

Another elbow from Davis silenced him.

"Julio," the woman went on, "please get Coapac."

Bolan and the RATs waited in silence. The Executioner glanced at Chambers and saw the confusion covering his face. The man still didn't want to believe that this woman had played him for a sucker. But now he was being hit squarely between the eyes with the fact. He had no choice but to face it.

"Coapac!" Josefa said a moment later. "I've been kidnapped!"

Bolan took the phone from her. "Hi, Rocha. Recognize the voice?" He didn't wait for an answer. "You told me earlier today we couldn't trade because I didn't have anything you wanted. I'd say things have changed. What would *you* say?"

There was a long silence at the other end of the phone. Then Rocha said, "I don't know the woman who just spoke to me."

"Sure you don't." Bolan handed the receiver back to Josefa. "He doesn't know you."

She ripped the instrument from his hand. A long stream of Spanish curses followed, then the woman said, "Coapac, they'll kill me if you don't cooperate with them!" She handed the phone back to Bolan.

"Recognize her now, Rocha?"

The drug lord let out a long breath on the other end. "What is it you want, Harkin?"

"You know what I want. I understand you've not only got the usual coke on hand, but a big shipment of ice. I'll take it all."

Rocha's voice trembled slightly as he spoke. "It has been spoken for already."

"Tough. Whoever it was will have to wait until next time."

There was a long pause on the other end of the line. Finally Rocha said, "It's ten million dollars."

"No problem," Bolan told him. "How about seven hundred and fifty thousand in cash? The rest we'll work out in merchandise. AKs, M-16s, maybe some Uzis or Ingram M-11s. You say what, when and where."

"I want M-16s and Ingrams," Rocha replied. "Don't attempt to cheat me. And if you harm one hair on her head—"

"Yeah, right. You'll do all kinds of mean things to me. Spare me the threats, Rocha, I've heard them before. You just play the game, and she won't get hurt."

"How long will it take you to get the cash?"

"I've got it now. We can make the exchange tonight."

Rocha paused. "No. Make it tomorrow afternoon. It will take me until then to get the shipment together."

Bolan stifled a chuckle. Rocha didn't need time to get the dope together. He needed time to assemble his men and set up the ambush he hoped would end this North American Research Center nightmare once and for all.

"Fair enough," the Executioner said. "Where?"

He knew where. Rocha would want the odds in his favor. He'd want to attack on familiar ground, which meant only one place.

"My compound. Green Hell."

"That's fine. But how do I get there?" Bolan listened quietly while the crime boss gave him directions deep within the Chaco.

"Bring Josefa with you," Rocha said when he'd finished. "If she isn't there, or harmed, there will be no transaction."

"She'll be there," Bolan promised. "But don't try anything. There'll be at least three men on her. They'll have orders that if anything breaks out, their first bullets go in her head."

The Executioner hung up. He took a seat in a stuffed armchair across from Josefa. "Just to set the record straight," he said. "What *is* your name?"

"Josefa. Maria is my... professional name."

Chambers's mouth dropped open.

"Let's see if I've got the rest right," Bolan said. "You planned to rip off Rocha on the drug deal. But you needed help. That's where Chambers came in." From the corner of his eye, he saw the agent lean forward, gripping his ankles in an upright fetal position. A combination of heartache and confusion covered his face as his head jerked rapidly up and down.

"Yes." She sneered at the devastated DEA agent. "As soon as we'd gotten the money, I'm afraid Alan would have met with a fatal accident. But he is a sniveling idiot. His weakness forced me to change my plans."

"And your contingency plan was to sell the information about us to Rocha," Bolan suggested. "Then bide your time until you found another sucker, another man who'd fall so madly in love with you that he wouldn't see through your scheme."

Josefa smiled knowingly at the Executioner. "Yes. And it would have been simple. Men are fools. All that a woman has to do is drop her panties and let them smell the scent. They become like children."

A sob came from the couch. "Maria, please don't talk like that. You . . . you loved me," he whispered.

Josefa turned toward him, her face revealing an expression of total loathing. Her lips curled in a sneer as she spoke. "You were the biggest fool of all."

Chambers's features twisted into an almost inhuman mask of pain.

Frog Davis looked away from him and stood up in embarrassment. He started toward the kitchenette. "Sure hate to miss any of this little minidrama," he muttered, "but I'm as thirsty as hell. Anybody else want a beer?"

No one answered, and Josefa went on. "There is another thing I have wanted to tell you for a long time, Alan." She leaned forward, and a wicked, sadistic smile replaced the repulsion on her face. "Sex with you was revolting. It was the most nauseating experience of my life, and I wanted to tell you many times. Now I can. I have nothing to lose."

Alan Chambers screamed, and his hand darted under the cuff of his trousers. The brown leather of an ankle holster appeared, and then a Smith & Wesson Chief's Special leaped into his fist. A split second later he screamed again as he pulled the trigger.

The .38 hollowpoint round drilled into Josefa Pescadora's face through the left eye socket. It threw her back against the couch, where she settled in a sitting position, the cruel grin on her face frozen for eternity.

Chambers stood. "I *loved* you," he raged. The .38 fell limply to the end of his arm.

Six men drew down on the crazed DEA agent. "Drop the gun, Chambers," Bolan ordered.

The man looked up, his eyes glazed as if he might be in a trance. He backed away from the couch to the wall, the gun still aimed at the floor.

"Drop it," Elliot said. "We don't want to hurt you, Alan."

Chambers's gaze traveled across the room, stopping briefly on Bolan, then each member of the RAT team. "I loved her!" he shouted.

Then he jammed the stubby .38 into his mouth and pulled the trigger.

THE THREE ARMY SUPPLY trucks rolled down the dirt road, crossing the great alluvian plain between the Paraguay River to the east and the Andes Mountains to the west.

For the most part, Green Hell appeared to support no life but scraggly scrub trees. But here and there forests, swamps and savannas spotted the bleak land. The convoy crossed an ancient wooden bridge, and thick timberland appeared in the distance.

"This must be the place," Elliot said from the passenger's seat of the lead truck. Like the rest of the RATs in the trailing trucks, the team leader wore desert cammies. A floppy jungle hat festooned with twigs and leaves had been pulled low on his brow. Elliot's Glock 17 and a "six-pack" of extra magazines hung in nylon from the belt around his waist. An M-16 lay across his lap.

The Executioner held his hand out the driver's window, and the convoy came to a halt. Lifting the microphone from the hook on the dash, Bolan thumbed the button. "We're almost there. Any last-minute problems?" He released the button.

Static buzzed from the radio, then a loud click sounded. Frog Davis came back from the truck behind Bolan. "We're in good shape here. How about you, Dow?"

From the third truck, Nolan Dow said, "I was born ready, Frog-face. Let's give 'em hell."

Bolan had grown to like the men of the RAT team during their brief time together. Elliot, Streck, Dow, Gober and Davis reminded him of his old Special Forces unit in Southeast Asia. They were typical of men who lived on the edge, knowing each breath they took might be their last. They cursed and insulted each other without mercy, but God help the man outside their "family" who tried the same.

The warrior threw the truck in gear, and the convoy crept slowly toward the forest. On the grassy plain that surrounded the trees, Bolan spotted a long landing strip.

Leaning across Elliot, the warrior flipped open the glove compartment and produced a small, black plastic transmitter. Roughly the size of a television remote control, the transmitter had only four buttons. The top button was green. The rest were red. A thumb switch reading On and Off was recessed into the right edge.

The Executioner flipped the switch to On. He dropped the transmitter into the breast pocket of his blacksuit as the convoy turned off the road down a narrow path through the trees. He thought back to the briefing he'd given the men the night before. Josefa Pescadora's untimely death had forced him to alter his plans, prompting both Davis and Gober to voice objections.

On the surface Bolan's new strategy did seem like suicide, and the RATs' apprehension was fine with the Executioner. Special Forces soldiers were trained differently than regular troops. They learned to think for themselves rather than blindly take orders. And as he'd continued to explain, the wisdom of the plan had sunk in.

Without the woman, they were back where they'd started. Rocha himself had summed it up.

They had nothing the Asunción crime boss wanted.

From here on in, they'd be running on pure, unadulterated bluff.

When the tall concrete wall appeared at the end of the road, the Executioner reached into his pocket and pressed the green button on the transmitter. He pulled the truck up to an alcove surrounding the gate.

Above him razor wire topped the ten-foot wall. Electronic cameras moved slowly back and forth on swivels just below the wire.

A speaker had been built into the wall on the driver's side. Bolan reached out the window and tapped the button.

"Come in, Señor Harkin," said a voice from the speaker.

The gate swung open, and Bolan pulled the truck into the compound.

Twenty men, ten on each side, aimed machine pistols at the trucks as they pulled to a halt in the center of a large courtyard. The Executioner's trained eyes quickly surveyed the compound. A large house—evidently Rocha's residence—sat against the wall opposite the gate. To the left was a long building that could only be barracks, and next to it was a shooting range. To the right Rocha's fleet of approximately thirty transport trucks was parked in line.

More armed men appeared from the barracks and circled the trucks. Snipers popped up on top of the house and barracks.

"Shit," Elliot muttered. "Just when you thought it was safe to go back in the water..."

A tall man with a ponytail walked out of the front door of the house toward the trucks, flanked by two hardmen.

Bolan recognized the man on the right as Domenguin.

The warrior lifted the MP-5 from the seat next to him, then he and Elliot exited the truck and walked to the front.

Rocha and his bodyguards came to a halt in front of him. Domenguin and the other man pointed Uzis at the Executioner's abdomen.

An insincere smile twisted the drug lord's thin lips as he extended his hand.

Bolan let it hang untouched. "I came to do business, not make friends."

Rocha dropped his hand, his face reddening slightly. "Where is Josefa?"

The warrior chuckled. "You don't think I'm that stupid, do you? She's nearby, safe. You'll get her just as soon as we're safe."

Rocha's eyes narrowed. "Harkin, if you have harmed—"

Bolan cut him off. "Seems I've heard this speech before. Why don't we get on with business?"

Slowly Rocha nodded. He turned to Elliot. "You and the rest of the men will stay here." Looking back at Bolan, he said, "Follow me."

Domenguin and the other bodyguard moved behind Bolan, their weapons now trained at his back. They brought up the rear as the Executioner followed Rocha into the house, through the living room and into a study lined with bookshelves.

Two Orientals sat in leather chairs next to the shelves. The taller of the men was slim, his skin stretched tightly across his face as if it might be too small for his body. The portly man munched happily on peanuts from a bowl on his lap.

Rocha didn't bother with introductions, but it was clear to the Executioner who they were.

The men in the leather chairs represented the Triad.

A dozen fifty-five-gallon drums stood on end in the middle of the room. Rocha pried the lid off one and reached into his pocket. Producing a small, stag-handled pocketknife, he cut through the plastic liner and lifted a small amount of white powder onto the blade. "Care to sample it, Señor Harkin?"

"No."

"The ice is in the barrels to the rear. Would you like to see it?"

Bolan chuckled. "No, thanks. I trust you."

"Then let us see your money and weapons."

Bolan followed Rocha back to the trucks. From somewhere in the distance came the sound of helicopter rotors.

The Executioner pulled the canvas curtain away from the rear of his truck, and Rocha peered in. His expression changed from surprise, to confusion, to anger when instead of rifles he saw thirty men in camouflage fatigues armed with M-16s.

Rocha was no fool. Bolan saw him sum up the situation, realize that all three vehicles must be "Trojan" trucks, weigh the odds and make his decision— all in a heartbeat.

The drug lord dived under the truck.

The first shot came from one of the drug guards in front of the barracks. Bolan turned, tapped the trigger of the MP-5 and sent a burst of 9 mm rounds through the gunner's face as the members of five RAT teams poured from the rear of the truck.

They were joined by sixty more men from the other two trucks as the courtyard lit up like the Fourth of July. Streck, Dow, Gober and Davis leaped from the cabs, their M-16s blazing.

Next to the Executioner, Elliot opened up with his own assault rifle, taking down Domenguin and his partner in one sweeping burst.

Bolan dropped to his belly, squirming beneath the truck after Rocha as thunder filled the sky. The drug lord rolled to his side, pulling a Detonics Scoremaster from his belt and tapping the trigger.

The quickly snapped round ricocheted off the underside of the truck and drilled into the dirt. Rocha wormed to the front of the truck and rose to his feet, bolting for the house.

The Executioner rolled to the edge of the vehicle. A steady stream of gunfire forced him back. From beneath the truck, he saw one of the new RATs take a round in the chest. The man went down, then got back up firing, the white ballistic nylon of his vest visible through his ripped fatigue blouse.

Crawling to the other side of the truck, Bolan rose to his feet in time to see Rocha push through the front door. The warrior sprinted after him. A round ripped through the shoulder of his blacksuit, and he felt the familiar burn of a shallow flesh wound.

Overhead the sound of whirling rotors filled the air. A half-dozen choppers hovered over the compound, their mounted .60-caliber machine guns mowing down Rocha's men as voices screamed over the PA systems: "DEA! Throw down your weapons!"

Bolan vaulted the steps and dived to his belly on the porch, two slugs from the Scoremaster sailing through the front door and over his head. Rocha turned and raced from the living room down the hall.

The Executioner pursued, dropping low as he barreled into the room. As more bullets sailed harmlessly past, Rocha disappeared behind a bookcase that had been pulled from the wall.

Bolan looked up to see the shocked faces of two Orientals. The fat man's hand reached for what had to be a gun hidden under the fat drooping over his belt.

The Executioner emptied the MP-5 in the man's chest and dropped the weapon to the floor.

As he drew the Desert Eagle, an automatic appeared in the thin Oriental's hand. Both men fired simultaneously. The Asian's round gouged along the side of the Executioner's thigh, taking a small strip of flesh with it.

Bolan's .44 hit the Oriental in the sternum, taking half his chest and his life.

The warrior sprinted to the bookshelf, the Desert Eagle leading the way. Peering around the corner, he saw the narrow closet and opened trapdoor.

He pulled the mini-flashlight from a pocket of his blacksuit and cautiously walked forward. A ladder from the top disappeared down into the darkness. Twisting the end of the flashlight, he shone the beam down into the hole.

A booming .45 winked in the darkness below before streaking through the opening to embed itself in the wall.

Bolan killed the light. From the darkness below, he heard rapid retreating footsteps. He stared through the hole. By now Rocha's eyes would have adjusted to the dim light of what had to be a tunnel. If he descended the steps of the ladder, he'd be no better off than a duck in a shooting gallery.

But the Executioner had no idea where the tunnel led. It might end at any point in Green Hell. By the time he located the exit, Rocha would be long gone. He dropped the magazine from the Desert Eagle and inserted a fresh load of .44s, took a deep breath and jumped.

The fall was less than four yards. Bolan's feet hit concrete, and he rolled to one side. Thunder boomed somewhere in front of him, and he saw the flash of the Detonics at the end of a long corridor.

Bolan returned the fire, shooting blindly toward the muzzle-flash. He heard more running footsteps, then the sound of rusty metal hinges.

Fresh air flowed into the tunnel. Light appeared in the distance, and he saw Rocha climbing another ladder.

The Executioner aimed the beam of the mini-flash down the tunnel and fired. The .44 Magnum hollowpoint round streaked along the tunnel and drilled Rocha in the left leg. The Scoremaster clattered to the ground. The drug lord lost his grip on the ladder and fell after it.

Bolan rose to his feet and sprinted down the tunnel. He thrust the beam of the flashlight into Rocha's face with one hand and pointed the Desert Eagle with the other.

Rocha's smile surprised him. The man clutched the bullet hole in his leg with both hands, then laughed. "Well, Señor Harkin, or whoever you are. It appears you have won this round." He paused, drawing in a breath that made him grimace painfully. The smile returned as he said, "You aren't a gunrunner, are you?"

"No."

"I didn't think so. It seemed I heard the letters DEA from the helicopters."

"Right again."

Rocha laughed, then sighed. "Then you will be reading me my rights, I suppose. And within a few hours I will make bond and be free again. And you must free Josefa."

"This time you're wrong. Josefa's already dead," the Executioner told him. "I'm not a member of any police force."

A brief look of perplexity crossed Rocha's face, then realization dawned. He was staring his executioner in the face. With a cry of animal rage, Rocha lunged at his adversary.

The Desert Eagle boomed in the confines of the tunnel. The force of the big Magnum slug punched Rocha back to the ground. He lay in a crumpled heap, open eyes staring lifelessly.

The reigning drug lord of Asunción was dead.

EPILOGUE

The firefight was over by the time the Executioner returned to the courtyard. The helicopters had landed next to Rocha's transport trucks. Weapons and the fallen bodies of Rocha's drug guards scattered the compound like discarded trash.

With the help of the several other RATs, Streck and Gober had herded the survivors to a corner of the compound. The few men who had wisely surrendered now squatted with their hands on their heads.

The RATs had sustained no casualties. Medics looked after the few who'd been wounded. The ballistic vests had protected their vital chest areas, and there'd been no head shots except a young man who'd been grazed across the forehead. He sat laughing and joking with Frog Davis as Bolan walked through the emergency cots that had been set up in the courtyard.

Elliot and Dow stood next to the truck Bolan had driven. Dow lit a cigarette as the Executioner approached. "You get the son of bitch?" he asked.

Bolan nodded. He glanced around the compound. "Let's finish the job."

Without speaking, they slid behind the wheels of the three trucks. Elliot parked his next to the house. Dow drove to the barracks, and Bolan's came to a halt in the middle of Rocha's fleet of transport trucks.

The roar of more big engines sounded outside the gate. Three Paraguayan army personnel vehicles pulled into the compound. The RATs standing guard over the prisoners pushed them up into the trucks before climbing aboard themselves. The rest of the men loaded the wounded.

Bolan walked to the gate. A young voice called to him from behind the wheel of one of the personnel carriers. "Hop in, sir. I'll give you a lift."

The warrior swung up into the passenger's seat and saw a redheaded kid of around twenty. Sergeant's stripes rode on the arms of his fatigues.

"Thanks. Let's get out of here, soldier."

An eerie silence hung over Green Hell as the transport trucks passed through the gate of the compound. When they had traveled down the narrow road a hundred yards, Bolan ordered the driver to the side of the road.

The other trucks passed.

Bolan stepped out of the vehicle and stared at the concrete walls of Rocha's compound. He pulled the transmitter from his blacksuit.

The green button had signaled the helicopters that the Executioner and the RAT teams had arrived at the compound, and it was time to move in.

Now it was time for the red buttons.

The warrior tapped the first button and heard an explosion behind the walls. Flames leaped from the rear of the compound where Coapac de la Rocha's house had once stood.

The second red button ignited the C-4 plastic explosives in the truck Elliot had parked next to the barracks. More fire rose over the concrete walls from the left side of the compound.

The Executioner pressed the final button and heard the explosion. Then a series of lesser charges erupted as one by one Rocha's cocaine transport trucks burst into flames.

Bolan climbed back aboard the personnel vehicle.

Coapac de la Rocha, and his alliance with the ice-dealing Chinese Triad, was a thing of the past. But the man known to the world as the Executioner didn't try to fool himself. It would only be a matter of time before someone else worked out a similar affiliation.

But when they did, they'd have Mack Bolan to deal with.

The Executioner stared at the thick trees of the forest within the wastelands known as Green Hell as his young driver threw the truck into gear.

"Let's go, Sergeant," the warrior said. "We've still got work to do."

Join Mack Bolan's latest mission in

THE TERROR TRILOGY

Beginning in June 1994, Gold Eagle brings you another action-packed three-book in-line continuity, the Terror Trilogy. Featured are THE EXECUTIONER, ABLE TEAM and PHOENIX FORCE as they battle neo-Nazis and Arab terrorists to prevent war in the Middle East.

Be sure to catch all the action of this gripping trilogy, starting in June and continuing through to August.

Book I:	JUNE	FIRE BURST (THE EXECUTIONER #186)
Book II:	JULY	CLEANSING FLAME (THE EXECUTIONER #187)
Book III:	AUGUST	INFERNO (352-page MACK BOLAN)

Available at your favorite retail outlets in June through to August.

Don't miss out on the action this summer— and soar with Gold Eagle!

TT94-1

Don't miss out on the action in these titles featuring
THE EXECUTIONER, ABLE TEAM and PHOENIX FORCE!

The Freedom Trilogy

Features Mack Bolan along with ABLE TEAM and
PHOENIX FORCE as they face off against a communist
dictator who is trying to gain control of the troubled
Baltic State and whose ultimate goal is world supremacy.

The Executioner #61174	BATTLE PLAN	$3.50	☐
The Executioner #61175	BATTLE GROUND	$3.50	☐
SuperBolan #61432	BATTLE FORCE	$4.99	☐

The Executioner ®

With nonstop action, Mack Bolan represents ultimate
justice, within or beyond the law.

#61178	BLACK HAND	$3.50	☐
#61179	WAR HAMMER	$3.50	☐

(limited quantities available on certain titles)

TOTAL AMOUNT	$
POSTAGE & HANDLING	$
($1.00 for one book, 50¢ for each additional)	
APPLICABLE TAXES*	$ _____
TOTAL PAYABLE	$ _____
(check or money order—please do not send cash)	

To order, complete this form and send it, along with a check or money order for the
total above, payable to Gold Eagle Books, to: **In the U.S.:** 3010 Walden Avenue,
P.O. Box 9077, Buffalo, NY 14269-9077; **In Canada:** P.O. Box 636, Fort Erie, Ontario,
L2A 5X3.

Name: _____

Address: _____ City: _____

State/Prov.: _____ Zip/Postal Code: _____

*New York residents remit applicable sales taxes.
 Canadian residents remit applicable GST and provincial taxes.

GEBACK5

A biochemical weapons conspiracy puts America in the hot seat. Don't miss

STONY MAN™

S E C R E T

ARSENAL

With a desperate situation brewing in Europe, top-secret STONY MAN defense teams target an unseen enemy. America unleashes her warriors in an all-out counterstrike against overwhelming odds!